LAVISH PRAISE
THE DANGEROUS
OF ALTAR BOYS

"The freshness of Chris Fuhrman's novel comes from his ability to squeeze out of a time of transition universal evocations of rebellion against growing up. . . . First-time events explode from the pages."

—Charles R. Larson, *Chicago Tribune*

"Brilliant, beautiful, heartbreaking. . . . The author's real triumph lies in the ability to plumb wild young minds, to reveal the ardent, romantic hearts that beat within wisecracking boys. Their wild, unself-conscious beauty permeates the book. We watch them navigate their lives at the precise moment when all their passionate wondering about life begins to yield secrets."

—Kate Tuttle, *Boston Book Review*

"A rollicking story set at a Catholic school in Savannah, Georgia . . . develops a series of sometimes hilarious vignettes on rebellion. [The] antics are not mere games, but life-affirming acts of defiance. . . . Imaginative and delightful adventures."

—Paul F. Young, *Los Angeles Reader*

"Read the opening lines of this feisty first novel, and you'll realize at once that you're in the hands of a storyteller with an arrestingly odd sense of drama. . . . The voice is fresh and assured. The setting . . . is a provocative mixture of traditional South, with all its baggage of old racial animosities and Civil War memories, and a brave, new, post-1960s world. [Fuhrman's] everything a promising first novelist should be—spirited and intuitive. . . . One can only regret that such a winning, lively voice was silenced just as it began to reach us."

—Michael Upchurch, *Atlanta Journal-Constitution*

The Dangerous Lives of ALTAR BOYS

A NOVEL BY CHRIS FUHRMAN

WASHINGTON SQUARE PRESS
PUBLISHED BY POCKET BOOKS

New York   London   Toronto   Sydney   Tokyo   Singapore

This book is for the FUHRMAN family, for CHRISANNE,
and for the gang

The life this novel enjoys as a published work is due in large part
to the dedication and tireless efforts of the author's friend and peer,
DAVID ELLIOT KIDD

"Thirteen," "The Usual Gang of Idiots," and "A Priest with a Girlfriend" were first published
in *Columbia: A Magazine of Poetry & Prose*, no. 17 (Fall 1991): 201–30.

This book is a work of fiction. Names, characters, places and incidents are products of the
author's imagination or are used fictitiously. Any resemblance to actual events or locales or
persons, living or dead, is entirely coincidental.

 WSP

A Washington Square Press Publication of
POCKET BOOKS, a division of Simon & Schuster Inc.
1230 Avenue of the Americas, New York, NY 10020

Copyright © 1994 by Chrisanne Fuhrman

Published by arrangement with The University of Georgia Press

Library of Congress Cataloging-in-Publication Data

Fuhrman, Chris.
   The dangerous lives of altar boys : a novel / by Chris Fuhrman.
     p.   cm.
   ISBN 0-671-52903-X
   1. Boys—Georgia—Savannah—Fiction. 2. Catholics—Georgia—
   Savannah—Fiction. 3. Savannah (Ga.)—Fiction. I. Title.
   [PS3556.U3245D36   1996]
   813′.54—dc20   95-36084
                                             CIP

First Washington Square Press trade paperback printing
February 1996

10 9 8 7 6 5 4 3 2 1

WASHINGTON SQUARE PRESS and colophon are
registered trademarks of Simon & Schuster Inc.

Cover design by Lisa Litwack

Printed in the U.S.A.

Thirteen

By eighth grade, Jesus Christ had been bone meal and rumors for most of 1,974 years, but we were only thirteen. We were daredevils, gangsters. I had a girl's name, Francis, and a hernia.

School and church occurred right down everybody's street at Blessed Heart, the two buildings joined at the shoulder by a glass bridge. My best friends, Tim and Rusty, were serving Mass that Sunday, kneeling on each side of the priest in their cassocks and wayward purple socks. I watched from the farthest pew, beside my mother. We'd been late again. To see the altar, I had to rock side-to-side behind the orchard of shifting heads.

Father Kavanagh was praying, his Irish mumble amplified by the PA system into the voice of God. He pinched the Host out of the chalice and raised it like a man admiring a silver dollar, Tim's cue to shake the bells. He thrashed them, brass clashing brass so harshly that heads flinched. Kavanagh flung Tim a thunderbolt glare. Tim stiffened his face.

Jesus hung crucified on the pink marble behind them, rolling up plaster eyes.

The bell signaled that the bread wafer in Kavanagh's fingers was now the flesh of Christ. You're supposed to be amazed, but

I was an altar boy too and had suffered Mass about three times a week for the last two years. It was no more mysterious or astounding to me than delivering newspapers had been. We called this the Magician's Assistant Syndrome. We were something like atheists by then.

Gathered behind a microphone to the left of the altar were two men with beards and guitars, an obese guy hunched over a piano, and a woman dangling a tambourine. They were there to make music for what the church was calling, in those days, a Folk Mass, an attempt at timeliness which I considered as pitiful as an adult using teenage slang.

Kavanagh raised the wine chalice in front of his face, gold cup haloed by steely hair, and turned it into Christ's blood. Tim rang the bells again, reasonably. I stopped listening. Some numb part of my brain answered the prayers for me.

Marjorie Flynn was kneeling in the pew ahead of me. Her wicked brother Donny was in my eighth-grade class. Margie had grown steadily beautiful all year without alerting the popular boys, and I'd been falling in love with her although we'd never spoken. I only knew that she'd been an honor student and shy and that last summer she had sliced her wrists with a razor blade. Something in her life was more important, more terrible, than anything in mine.

Margie wore a sleeveless white silk dress so fresh and pretty it caused my stomach to ache. She was pale, but rosy around the eyes, nose, and cheeks, as if she stayed indoors all the time, crying, an image I found appealing.

The rear doors of the church were open, and a honeysuckle breeze came in and proved itself on Margie's hair. She wore it curly and wild. All the other girls wore their hair straight, rolling it around orange juice cans or ironing it somehow. Margie's looked careless, gorgeous.

Across the aisle Melissa Anderson, head full of bows, spread the fingers of both hands and admired her nails. Our athletes bloodied each other's noses over this specimen, that year's May Queen, as if I cared, and she certainly never wasted a thought on boys like me. But for Margie I would've done anything, though she didn't seem like the type to require that. I wanted to protect her from something, anything. I bowed my head and inhaled, trying to smell her, but the aromas of church interfered, incense, flowers, and perfume.

Beside us, the windows caught sunlight and thickened it into burning colors, stenciling the carpet with sacred symbols in reverse and the names of dead patrons thrown backwards. Serpents and winged lions and unicorns fell from the glass, sprawled in the aisles. The dragon window was my favorite. I knew the air bubbles in every jigsaw pane. Saint George, in armor, had sunk a lance into the dragon's belly and rested his booted foot on its back. I pitied the dragon, but I envied his slayer's heroics.

In an elaborate, blood-spattered daydream I rescued Margie Flynn from an alligator that crawled out of the pond across the street. She tore a strip from her hem, baring her thighs, to clean my wounds.

Meanwhile, Father Kavanagh had arrived at the part where he told us to "offer each other a sign of peace" and you shook hands with people you ordinarily ignored and said, "Peace be with you." I began praying for Margie to turn and take my hand, godless convictions suspended for the moment. I angled slightly towards my mother to appear unconcerned. The old man on the other side poked my arm, and I was obliged to pump his soft, damp hand while he stared at my mother.

I turned back, and Margie was glancing at me, then the old man reached over in front of me and caught Mama's hand and petted it, grinning. There would've been an awkward, desperate stretch to get to Margie. She turned forward. My heart flattened. Then Mama gave the old guy a shame-on-you wink and retrieved her hand. She touched Margie's shoulder, and then they

3

shook. Margie's eyes bumped mine. She held her hand out to me, her wrist fragile as a swan's throat and crossed with a thin white scar which caused that pain in my sinuses like I was about to cry. I took her hand. She looked away. Then she looked at me, and our eyes locked, and the tiniest smile possible passed over her face, barely entering her eyes. My mind drained. She said, "Peace be with you," then my name. I watched her say, "Francis," and liked hearing it for the first time in my life. Her hand in mine felt like something radioactive.

Her fingers slid away, and she drew back and turned towards the altar. My eyes fell from the golden hair, along the bare shoulders and down the new curves of her hips to the white-stockinged, rounded calves. I bunched my hands in my pockets to disguise the embarrassing extra. I wanted to run out alone and spend hours thinking about her, carve our initials into something. Her actual presence seemed like too much to bear for now. Every time I looked at her, my heart went off.

My mother was smiling at me. I frowned. We chanted with the priest, "Lamb of God who taketh away the sins of the world, have mercy on us," three times, rapping our breasts at each mention of the lamb. I was vigorous, producing a healthy thump.

Kavanagh unclipped his microphone necklace, causing electronic thunder.

The folk musicians began the Communion hymn. It was a popular folk song that I liked, and they played so well it startled me. The plump guy's fingers rippled at the keyboard, the bearded men started strumming, chords chiming in and out of the wood with the piano's sweet notes rolling all around it, then one man began to sing crisply, the girl rang the tambourine against a swaying hip, and behind the singer the other three mouths moved with a single shape and harmony, and I thought, God, what wonderful creatures humans are. My neck hair rose like a thousand needles.

And then something ran past our pew. A black dog.

This large, slippery-looking mongrel padded up the aisle along the wall. The ushers were surprised out of their hands-behind-the back poses and began to walk after the dog. The dog slipped through rainbow pools of light, tags clinking, then rolled near the altar rail and paddled its ribs with a hindleg. It was obviously male. The priests and deacon ignored it. The heads were all bobbing, and I could see between them, the dog panting, cartoon eyes wide. His tongue melted out over his teeth and slobber trickled off. Rusty and Tim's cheeks hollowed and their lips disappeared.

An usher with an overgrown mustache grabbed for the dog's collar, and the dog torpedoed down the center aisle, pausing halfway to insert his snout under a woman's dress and throw his head. The usher's mustache stretched in amused apology. He genuflected at the altar rail and came towards the dog, the others following, bent over as if that made them invisible. I watched Margie watch them. Her eyes narrowed into bright slices.

The dog leapt past the crouching ushers and ran towards the altar again, and the men turned like a wave. They would've had to sprint to catch him. The dog slunk under the altar rail, swinging his head back to watch for them. Father Kavanagh and young Father O'Leary stood over the dog, ready to give Communion. People began to rise. The dog put his nose to a railing post and snuffled, spun around, crooked his hindleg, and the priests skipped aside, and the dog squirted a glittering stream that spattered the marble, darkening a circle into the creamy carpet beneath. He stared gloomily out at us, mouth open. The congregation hung back. There was nice music underneath all this.

Tim jammed a fist against his mouth and sputtered behind it. Rusty turned his back, vibrated. Kavanagh shifted the chalice, stepped forward, and swept his hand back like a bowler and slapped the dog's rump so hard that the animal jumped

5

the railing and slid into the aisle yelping, popping his eyes, and bounded past the ushers and out the doors. The ushers closed them behind him and the wind died.

Father O'Leary's eyes slid towards Kavanagh. Kavanagh's jaw was rigid. O'Leary squeezed the smile from his own lips.

I laughed in an excruciating whisper, the edge of my watery gaze on Margie. My hernia was aching. I opened my mouth and breathed. My mother was peering over a missalette, eyes huge, then she snorted and pressed it around her face. Margie's hands were steepled over her mouth, hiding, I was sure, a grin. The musicians had used up all their lyrics and were playing instrumental. The first-row people began to kneel along the altar rail as a line formed in the aisle.

I rose, leaving two craters in the cushioned kneeler, and squeezed past my mother to follow Margie up to Communion. A man wedged between us, poisonous with after-shave. Twice I saw the corner of Margie's eye, as if her attention was directed back at me. The people kneeling left a gap, marked by the deacon's handkerchief, where the dog had puddled. I shuffled up and kneeled one place down from Margie and tilted my face up. Like a celebrity, her presence made everything else small.

Kavanagh sidestepped to me, held the Eucharist out like a tidbit, and said, "The body of Christ." Rusty, holding the paten under my chin to catch holy crumbs, had blanked his face, but his neck swelled with plugged-up laughter. I said, "Amen," and the priest laid the wafer on my tongue.

I followed Margie back to the rear. Her style of walking made me feel weak. I kept my head bowed while an usher slid the second collection in front of me, full of paper money and envelopes with families' names on them. Mama had dropped our single quarter in the first basket. Daddy, broke, had stayed home with my brothers in protest of the church's materialism.

I held the Eucharist in my teeth, away from tongue and saliva. We played this game to see how long we could keep it from dis-

6

solving. A strange thrill resulted from keeping the alleged Jesus trapped in your teenage mouth.

The folk song ended with the guitar picks scratched slowly across the strings, and a final chord shimmered out and died beautifully with the piano trembling down around it into a final humming that seemed to make sense out of the world. The microphone whined briefly. Margie's shoulders lifted, with a breath, and relaxed.

Kavanagh sliced a cross into the air with his hand, blessing us in the name of the Father and of the Son and of the Holy Ghost (younger priests always said Spirit). Two-hundred voices amened. I didn't, because I still had solid Jesus in my mouth, breaking all my records.

"The Mass is ended," Kavanagh said, "go in peace." Then he hugged the podium and made announcements, asked for money and volunteers. Rusty and Tim carried cruets of water and wine into the sacristy. Out of sight, they'd suck down most of the wine. They'd be pouring a few innocent drops into the storage bottle when Kavanagh got there.

The musicians began to play "Dominique," a silly tune from the movie *The Singing Nun,* but instead of singing the words they exchanged guarded, ironic looks.

The rest of the day belonged to me. It was paid for now.

Everybody paraded towards the doors. They dipped two fingers each in the font of holy water at the vestibule and dabbed themselves with the sign of the cross: forehead, breastbone, left shoulder, right. I reached into my pocket and palmed my rabbit's foot, dunked it into the water as I passed, increasing its magic and trade value.

Outside was so bright my eyes ached. Sun blazed up from honeysuckle shimmering with bees, from yellow brick and palms and old grass, and in front of me, Margie Flynn's hair bouncing with each click of her heels on pavement.

Mama stopped to trade complaints with Mrs. Doolan, a thick-legged neighbor who was always swollen with babies. Her husband worked Sundays, a cop. Margie stood beside her mother, who was talking to Father O'Leary near the sidewalk. I wanted to say something to her so badly it was like a hand squeezing the back of my neck, but I couldn't think of anything that didn't sound stupid or pathetic. Already, I doubted anything had been shared. I'd been looking at it all through a microscope, as usual.

Tim and Rusty would be coming out the back way soon. I started towards the corner of the church, past the black dog licking himself shamelessly near a family that wouldn't look at him. I turned for a final glimpse of Margie Flynn. She was looking at me. We looked down. I watched my shoes press grass, and then, as I turned the corner, I periscoped back to dare another look, and she caught me again. She smiled and raised her hand, sprinkling her fingers at me, and her fingers might've been brushing my heart.

The body of Christ dissolved in my mouth, a gooey melt of starch, and I swallowed him, happy, miserable, in distant love.

The Usual Gang
of Idiots

Homeroom next morning smelled of cough drops. Nearly summer, nobody had a sore throat. But gum was forbidden. Cough drops were classroom candy. Even the nuns sucked them.

Sister Ascension, the principal, lumbered in and whispered to our teacher, Sister Rosaria, who bobbed her head. Ascension called the names of our whole gang—Tim, Rusty, Wade, and me—along with her nephew, Joey O'Connor, and absolved us from classes to create a final drawing for the bulletin board in the hallway. The teachers knew our gang as artists more than outlaws.

Ascension relayed us to the library, beside her office. The librarian, Miss Harper, led us back into the supply room. Miss Harper was as old as my grandma and had a wooden leg. She rolled her right side to accomplish every other step. She never smiled.

Miss Harper took shears from a drawer and stood beside a table mounted with a wide roll of paper. Tim and I, on each side, pinched a corner of the paper and walked backwards, unscrolling it cracklingly, just longer than a bulletin board. Miss Harper's shears munched neatly across. Rusty and Joey rolled it up and we cut another piece.

Her mouth tight as a slot, Miss Harper surrendered her scis-

9

sors to Wade, the tallest, and a ration of thumbtacks to Joey, the fattest. Rusty and I carried the paper tubes. Miss Harper waited for us to leave ahead of her. Tim snatched a large book from one of the shelves and snuck it out to the hallway.

"Did you ever consider," said Tim, "that Miss Harper is about one-fourth wood? I wonder if it floats when she takes a bath?" Tim Sullivan was the smallest boy in our class, and the smartest. He'd been born here in Georgia, but lived several years up North. In his first week at Blessed Heart, he'd passed me a note that said GOD IS A LIE. REMEMBER SANTA CLAUS? Forming a gang was his idea, after he'd read *The Godfather*.

We smoothed the first paper roll across the upper part of the bulletin board, sank tacks through the corners into cork, and trimmed the edge. We overlapped the paper on the bottom and did the same. We stepped back and leaned on the aluminum railing that overlooked the cafeteria-gym-auditorium.

"It goes without saying," Tim said, "this won't be a normal drawing. This is our legacy to the school." He hawked and spit on the polished floor and mashed it under his shoe, then opened the big book and tapped an illustration. "Gustave Doré. Wild, hunh?"

In the engraving, muscular men and roundish women, all naked, writhed in a rocky pit, struggling with serpents which hid the men's privates. It was beautiful and dark and the detail carried into the distant crags, heaped with lost souls, snakes.

"They want religion, we'll do it right."

"Isn't this Gothic style?" I asked, showing off.

"This guy knew anatomy," Wade said. "I bet he dissected a corpse or two." Wade spoke in a voice deeper than his true voice. He was tall, muscular.

Rusty, a football player who hated his teammates, said, "I don't think they're gonna let us draw titties and all that."

Tim flipped to the index, then to an etching of the crucifixion. "Only on Mr. Jesus. Tastefully done."

We decided what supplies we'd need and went for them

while Tim and Wade began the outline with yellow pencil-nubs. We passed a seventh-grade classroom and the word "integers" seeped out of a vent and I was happy to be in the hallway and free, though in the last row, beside an aquarium flickering with orange fish, I knew Margie Flynn was warming the seat of her desk, possibly thinking of me at that exact moment.

Rusty, Joey, and I returned with the materials. We watched Tim and Wade. They skewed the angle of the drawing so it gazed up at Jesus from one side. Tim drew everything on the diagonal instead of amateurishly head-on. Joey wedged his bulk between Tim and Wade and began to rough in the motto Ascension had assigned (Christ has Died, Christ is Risen, Christ will Come Again). Tim trailed his pencil across the paper, glancing at the book every few seconds. He slowed down for the heads and hands, frowned at the point of his wriggling pencil.

He sketched in graceful streaks that became the folds of gowns, the hewn edges of crosses. Rusty and I moved in and boldened the outlines with Magic Markers. Tim fetched a wastebasket from the lavatory, turned it over, and stood on it to draw the crown of thorns. Bloodier than the original.

We swarmed the paper. All else vanished. Pencil lines became ink, ink grew into shadow, raw paper remained as light. Color squeaked in from markers and crayons and chalk. The lettering thickened, spiked with points and tails. We molded cross-hatching to the curves of the figures.

Father Kavanagh approached from the glass bridge, bringing the world back to us. He stopped and slid a pack of cigarettes from his breast pocket, shook one out and lit it with a square, silver lighter that plinked when he closed it. He watched us. He blew several tight smoke rings and tapped a manila envelope against his thigh. Then he turned and walked down the hall and knocked on our homeroom door and went inside to teach Religion class. The last smoke ring dilated and kneaded itself into wisps.

We worked. The paper got heavy with ink and sagged. We

refastened it. Tim ran back and forth between the bathroom and Jesus, checking the mirror, drawing his own face beneath the beard. We gave the soldiers the faces of Kavanagh and the nuns. We made ourselves the disciples. Giggling, Joey crucified the pope next to Christ, as a thief. Wade hung Alfred E. Neuman, *Mad*'s idiot coverboy, on the third cross. Beards and helmets kept it from being obvious libel.

The smell of sizzling burgers rose humidly from the cafeteria. My stomach rumbled. Joey's rumbled louder.

Rusty said, "We'd best slow down or we'll be finished before Second Lunch."

We stood back and looked at what we'd drawn, dark against the white painted cinder block. Down the way, Ascension walked across to our room and came out with Craig Dockery, a mean black kid, and took him into her office. Craig reemerged with a giant, empty bottle from the water cooler, slapping it like a drum. He stopped near us, lifted his chin, and cocked his head. "Y'all can't draw black people?"

Tim said, "This is Jerusalem in the year 33."

Craig said, "They had them back then." He swaggered slowly into the stairwell and it echoed with the boom of the big bottle.

Tim made Judas look like Craig.

When Craig came back, arms bulging with the weight of a full water bottle, he laughed through his nose. "You all right, Tiny Tim." He took the water into the principal's office.

Tim, who did not like being called tiny, said something vile. He turned back to us and said, "This is the last bulletin board. It needs magic."

Tim reached into his back pocket and took out a small knife. He opened the blade and it locked into place, click. "Got your lighter, Rusty?"

Rusty produced a butane lighter, flicked his thumb, and a flame spurted up. Tim turned the blade in it, then pulled it back and shook the heat out.

The bell rang above the bulletin board, jangling me.

Tim folded his left hand to his shoulder, raising the elbow. He pressed the knife to the skin underneath the elbow and pulled the blade across. I winced. No blood. He sliced again, then milked the skin and a couple of beads oozed out. "Eek," he said. He stepped up on the wastebasket and dabbed specks onto Christ's thorn-punctured head.

Voices echoed into the cafeteria, then filled it, as the younger kids arrived for First Lunch, hundreds of shouting mouths. A few tilted their heads back, watched us for a moment, nudged their friends, and pointed, then returned to their burgers and screaming.

Tim passed the knife to Rusty. Rusty's scalp and ears lifted slightly. But then he held his hand up and casually jabbed the web between thumb and forefinger, pressed it to the nailed hands, and smeared a thin line like cough-drop drool.

I couldn't cut myself. Tim offered. I closed my eyes and pinched my thigh to divert myself while Tim sliced behind my elbow, producing a token dribble. I made my mark on the skewered feet.

"Blood brothers to Jesus," Tim said, wiggling his eyebrows.

"I'm not doing it," Joey said. "Forget it."

"So save your blood," Tim said. "Who asked you?"

Wade sliced his left thumb, then looked shocked. Blood ticked to the floor. He cursed. He trickled blood on the nail holes, the crown of thorns, and the wounded side, then stepped back and flung droplets at the paper. "Damn! It's still coming out!" He sucked air through his teeth to show us that it hurt.

"Another day of Art," Tim said. "You better let the nurse take a look at that."

Wade went and told the nurse he'd gotten a freak paper-cut. He returned with his thumb padded in gauze and surgical tape.

Joey slid his chubby hands into his pockets.

†

Kavanagh emerged from the classroom, lit a cigarette, and wandered towards us. He stood at our backs and we stopped joking and exaggerated the drawing process. Kavanagh coughed. I peeked at him under my drawing arm. He was holding the manila envelope.

"You boys are the artists," he said, smoke cascading from his mouth, some of it threading back up into his nostrils.

Everybody turned around.

"Yes, Father," said Wade in his enhanced, deep voice.

"You are—Mr. Madison, correct?" Father Kavanagh pinched the cigarette to his lips and his cheeks caved in. The cigarette reddened and half an inch of ash grew there.

"Yes, Father."

"And Mr. Doyle?"

"Yes, Father," I admitted.

The steely haired priest nodded at us several times. He huffed out a cloud of smoke and unclasped the big envelope. "I'd like your opinion on this."

He slid out a sheaf of paper divided into bright comic-book panels. I'd colored them myself. I got the hot, giddy feeling of being in serious trouble, like just before a whipping.

"Is this familiar, Mr. Scalisi?" Kavanagh passed it to Rusty, who accepted as if it were a loaded rattrap.

We'd spent an entire weekend devising *Sodom vs. Gomorrah '74*, a spoof of our torments at Blessed Heart. It had disappeared from Wade's desk a few days before. We'd suspected Donny Flynn, Margie's brother. The last page showed the priests defiling fat, nude Sisters of Mercy on the church altar while our comic-book selves watched in horror from the choir loft.

We traded Death Row grimaces. Kavanagh's face was vague with smoke. I swallowed a horrible urge to laugh. We'd be ex-

14

pelled from school in disgrace, we'd have to run away from home.

Rusty, his face a struggle between shock and hilarity, slowly crumpled the pages in his fist while he stared out over the railing behind Kavanagh. The priest took it from him. "Oh no, don't destroy it. One of your classmates thought enough of it to drop it in the rectory mail slot." He smoothed out the crimps, ashes tumbling from his cigarette, and returned it to the envelope. Kavanagh's name was scrawled on the outside.

"What will your mothers think, I wonder? I believe it meets even the legal definition of obscene."

The hallway changed. The floor tilted like in a fun house, but instead of sliding I floated, unable to feel my body. The cafeteria chimed with forks and knives, trays rasped on tabletops, elfin voices enclosed us. Kavanagh's collar, between black bands, was bone white, radiant. He put the last of the cigarette to his lips and it glowed fiercely. He dropped it to the floor and pressed his toe on it. He exhaled smoke for a long, long time, and it lingered, curling and billowing in tendrils that finally became a haze.

Joey began clearing his throat, overdoing his usual nervous tics, snorting, grunting. Though not officially in the gang, he'd participated.

"Did you boys learn this sort of thing from magazines? Rock songs?" asked Kavanagh.

"No, Father," Tim said, discarding a fine excuse. The nuns thought "Bridge Over Troubled Water" was brainwashing us to shoot heroin. Things like that.

"Where then?"

Everyone stood paralyzed for a few seconds.

Then Rusty dropped his chin to his chest and said, "I guess we just picked it up off the street."

"You should've left it there."

I looked through the railing grid down into the cafeteria. The teachers were lining the children up, marching them outside.

15

"I ought to be shocked," said the Irish priest.

Tim asked—and I wanted to fling him over the railing—"Would this be a mortal sin, Father?"

Kavanagh's mouth was hard, as if he had nipped something in his front teeth, then he relaxed into a faint cynical smile that I'd never seen before. "Venial," he said, accompanied marvelously by smoke, though the cigarette had been dead a full minute. "In all probability, venial."

I had a moment's scared affection for him, as I sometimes had for my own father.

Metal doors crunched shut, and the last of the children's voices ceased. The awful silence tightened my shoulders and back, made me want to yell, run. The lunch bell clangalanged just behind my head and I jerked like a live wire had touched me, ducking and throwing my hands up, and all the others jumped and even Kavanagh was halfway to protecting his face. The bell stopped and left me shaking. I was thankful I hadn't cursed. The hallway narrowed with the opening of doors and our classmates poured out noisily and the teachers bunched together and I stared amazedly at Margie Flynn's face as it smiled past mine, became the back of a beautiful head, and turned the corner. The gang affected poses of relaxation. Kavanagh looked towards the teachers, held the envelope behind his back in both hands, waggling it. Joey blinked like a machine, grunted, sniffed.

"I'll ponder this over the next few weeks, regarding your graduation," Kavanagh said. He slit his eyes at the bulletin board. "It's hard to believe he'll rise after a crucifixion that gory, boys." He nodded at the teachers, then walked to the glass bridge, and the manila envelope was the last thing to disappear.

Joey pounded into the lavatory.

Tim, Rusty, Wade, and I gaped at one another. Faces pale, or red. Eyes wide or squinted. And then we began to laugh wildly, and the teachers scowled at us as they paused to survey the drawing, and Rusty doubled over in an agony of compressed laughter, farted like a buffalo, and the teachers pretended not to have heard and drifted away. Our laughter stabbed in breathless spasms as our classmates flowed around us.

†

Rusty and Tim were eating from paper cones filled with french fries, mustard-slathered. I sat across from them and stared at my hamburger. My stomach was queasy and I began to think about burgers, beef, cows in the slaughterhouse spilling out their bowels, and my thirty-five cents was wasted. Wade poured barbecue potato chips into his mouth from a large bag he'd brought. Joey was still upstairs in the bathroom, locked in a stall, moaning.

Every minute or so Tim and Rusty would titter and then everybody would catch it, laughing convulsively, mouths filled with mush. Finally we became exhausted. Wade folded his potato chip bag into a football and flicked it into a dive across the aisle and into a trash barrel. Margie was sitting down there on the girls' side. Our gazes crossed and something jammed in my stomach and then spread, that pleasant ache.

I looked up above her, into the other dimension of the hallway, and saw our mural of the gothic Christ, his wounds brown-smudged with our blood, the same that beat confusedly in my own heart.

"We're going to be thrown out of school," I said. "Margie's going to think I'm trash, a pig."

"I have a plan to save us," Tim said. "We're going to be legendary."

Miss Harper was slowly hobbling past our mural. She did not look at it. She leaned on her cane, rolled the leg forward, stepped. Suddenly I felt tremendously sorry for her, and my throat tightened and I had to blink.

17

✝

All the boys were playing softball. Our gang, though, was sprawled around the big oak tree, for a meeting. Every few minutes I looked up to see Margie, far away on the bleachers, talking to another girl. I invented their conversation, inserted myself as topic. On the soccer field an old man swept a metal detector in front of him, a wire running from the disk, up the handle, and into his earplug. Birds peeped above us.

Tim slid his fingers behind his ears and flipped longish blond hair out over them. He beat the regulations by slicking it back. He laid down his copy of *The Call of the Wild,* then growled and spit. "Goddamn allergies," he said. Then, "There's Joey. Hey, Joey!"

Fat Joey O'Connor ambled over, his eyeglasses blinding me until he entered the shade and I saw his eyes twitching behind the lenses. Sweat blotched under his arms, hair stuck to his brow in slashes. He shook his head, astonished.

"I'm dead. We won't graduate," he moaned. "I just had a bad episode in the bathroom."

"Have a seat," Tim said. "We've already got an exit from this situation."

I was arranging green cubes of bottle glass into a mosaic in the dirt. Rusty, slumped against the trunk, methodically scraped his orthopedic shoes on a big root that looked poured onto the ground like lava. Wade squeezed a pair of handgrips, his forearms bulging and vein-etched, his thumb-bandage stained.

"I'm not part of your damned 'gang,'" Joey said. "I'm not doing anything illegal."

The year before, we'd tried to recruit Joey because he could draw and was blasphemous and knew a lot about music. But he refused to steal or risk fights.

"Joey," Tim sighed, "your signature's on the evidence. You're worse off than us because Ascension's your aunt."

Joey looked like he'd been stabbed. "I—I was drunk when I drew it."

"So were we. Tell her that."

Joey groaned and let himself collapse onto an oak root. His lower lip quivered. I always felt boy-tough in Joey's presence, but shamefully so, like feeling good about yourself when you see somebody in a wheelchair.

"We're going to capture a mountain lion and release it in Blessed Heart School," Tim said.

The squeaking of Wade's handgrips stopped. I laughed.

"Francis thinks I'm bullshitting," Tim said.

Rusty said, "We got it worked out. Semi."

Wade and Joey said, "Mountain lion?"

I snickered some more. Tim stared at me patiently.

"We'll do the reconnaisance tomorrow," he said. "On the field trip. They have panthers there."

Rusty's mom was class mother, and she'd arranged an outing to Marshland Island, a new educational facility that included a sort of zoo. Rusty and Tim had suggested it.

"We can steal the cat on a Saturday," Tim said. "Then we bust into the school on Sunday and set it loose. We leave notes at the rectory and the convent saying what we've done. They'll close the school down until they catch it, and by then Kavanagh will have forgotten about our comic book. Compared to a rampaging wildcat, it'll seem like high jinks, see? It's relative. Like if you get bitten by a snake, you forget about the mosquito bite you got earlier."

Joey kept shaking his head, wiping sweat from his face with dirty hands, leaving streaks. He sniffled and grunted.

"The cops'll shoot it and we won't miss any school," Wade said.

"No," said Rusty. "It's an endangered species and it's government property. And first they've got to find it—we're talkin about a fuckin lion—and that'll take time, experts, equipment."

"What if they don't believe the notes?" I asked. "Suppose they have school anyway and somebody gets eaten? Jesus."

"The island will report the cat missing," said Tim. "There'll be obvious signs that we've tampered with a door or window. Et cetera."

"What if they catch it the first day?" Wade asked.

"Then we leave a new set of notes saying there's a bunch of rattlesnakes in the school now, or scorpions or whatever. After a cougar, they can't afford to doubt anything."

I said, "Even if we could do this, it seems cruel to the animal, and a hell of a lot of trouble."

"The problem with life," Tim explained, "is that when you're not in trouble it's boring."

"After the cat sees what's here—all the people and concrete and cars and all—he'll be glad to return to the island. He'll live out his life knowing he's in a good place." Rusty inflated his chest and folded his arms across it.

"And this is probably the last big job we'll ever do as a gang. After this summer, we'll probably never see each other again. We might as well finish up with something spectacular."

"I'm ready for it," Rusty said. "I don't give a shit anymore. I've lived a full life." Rusty's dad had been promoted to vice president of a lumber company whose home office was in Tennessee. After graduation, Rusty and his mom were moving up there.

"I spent a day in the juvenile home last summer," I said. "Remember? And this is more serious than ripping off Kmart."

"You surrendered," Tim said. "You did the genteel Robert E. Lee thing instead of hauling ass like the rest of us."

"Y'all are psychos," Joey hissed. He twitched, grunted. "Forget it. Don't even think about including me." He pulled himself up.

"And I can't do all the swashbuckler crap anymore," I said. "My hernia's gotten worse."

"We're artists," said Tim, meaning outlaws. "What would Picasso do in a situation like this? This is our last year. We can't just fade away."

Besides Rusty leaving, it seemed Wade's mother would marry

20

the architect she was dating and move Wade with her to South Carolina. My parents were saving to send me to Benedictine, the local military school run by monks. Tim was going North to prep school.

"This'll be good for all of us, and it'll prevent us from getting expelled."

"I need to think about it," I said. Tim grimaced.

"Not me," said Joey. "Hell no." He wiped under both eyes. Twin dirt smudges.

"Remember that panel you drew?" Tim said. "Kavanagh flogging Ascension's bare ass with the cat-o'-nine-tails?"

"No! No, no, no!" Joey hustled away, thighs slapping against each other.

Rusty made a meowing noise.

Mrs. Barnes stood in the field and shook a hand bell that meant recess was over. The softball games stopped, one side cheering, backslapping, the other side swearing and abusing the equipment. Boys stuffed their shirttails in and cinched their ties and milled into a rambling line where the girls were already gathered. We collected at the rear and began to trudge back to Blessed Heart. The man with the metal detector was on one knee, turning over sod with a minispade.

We passed the sandy area where the swing sets and slides were, then entered the near field. A white duck waddled towards us from the pond on the other side. Another duck scooted after it, nipping at its neck with his bright orange bill and trying to climb on its back. The rear of the line giggled and snickered, marched towards the intersection. Mrs. Barnes and most of the students had already been ushered across by red-belted patrol boys with the power to stop traffic.

Craig Dockery, tallest of the black boys, trotted out from the line and raised a baseball bat. He ran at the male duck. The duck whirled, scampered. Craig hit the duck and something popped. The duck squawked and flung itself in circles, dragging one wing.

"Got that motherfucker," Craig said. He laughed, deep-voiced. It was unbelievable. We didn't know what to do.

Rusty put his hands on his hips and dropped his mouth open. "Aw, what the hell'd he do that for?"

Therese Parker, the girl who kept a pet raccoon, ran after the duck. The duck flapped towards the pond. She followed, plaid skirt swishing.

I wanted to murder Craig, but I was suddenly very aware of my hernia, like a burr in my groin, and my knees were shaking and I felt weak. I watched Therese and the squalling duck. Something flashed beside me. I stumbled out of the way. Tim was on Craig's back, his arm around the boy's throat. Tim fumbled in his knife pocket. Rusty stepped over to stop him, and Craig grabbed the back of Tim's shirt and bent over and flung Tim down at Rusty's feet.

Tim jumped up, face flaming, and stood rigid with his fists out. Craig made a show of looking him up and down. Rusty lunged forward and Craig raised the bat. Rusty froze. Wade stood behind him, fists balled with the bandaged thumb flagging up. I realized it was just our gang and the black eighth-grade boys. The others had all gone in.

Tim panted, hair splayed out over his ears, grass stains on his back.

"Ain't nothin but a nasty old duck," Craig said. "It wasn't Donald Duck, little man."

Tim screamed a catalog of obscenities, conspicuously leaving out anything racial. The variety and combinations shocked us all. Craig's face slackened.

"Put the goddamn bat down," Rusty said, pointing jerkily, excited. "Mess with somethin your own size."

"This doesn't make sense," I said.

Lewis Epps, a boy so dark his skin looked blue in the sunlight, said, "Let's go, Craig. You're in the wrong, man."

Across the field, Therese was creeping towards the duck, baby-talking. The duck huddled against the fence of the swimming pool.

Tim forced a short, disgusted laugh, then spit near Craig's shoe. "Be glad I'm not carrying a gun. You're on my list, Dockery."

Craig raised his chin, squeezed the bat handle. "You just itchin to call me a nigger, ain't it? That's what you're thinkin."

"No I am not," Tim sneered.

"Nigger donkey-dick sucker!" said Rusty.

"Lovely." Tim rolled his eyes. "Let's have a little race riot." He pushed his hair back behind his ears and stalked off towards Therese and the duck.

Nobody said anything else. I hated Craig, and I had to force myself not to let it spread to the guys behind him and to all black people, the way you might hate all dogs, say, if you'd been bitten a couple of times. I saw it in their eyes too, something that didn't have much to do with any of us, but did. We looked the same to them, maybe, as the men blasting their people with fire hoses in the old news films. They looked the same as the occasional boys that robbed me and called me honky or cracker boy while they did it.

I made myself think of some of the black families on my old paper route, and the ugliness buried itself a little.

Therese Parker ran past us, muddy knees, tear-striped face, and we sulked towards school, wearing identical green uniforms, but divided according to the parts that showed, hands and faces, pink or brown.

23

✝

Tim joined us later at the bulletin board. He said Therese had gotten Sister Ascension to call the Humane Society and that he'd guarded the duck until they arrived in an old station wagon. They gave the duck an injection and took it away to the animal hospital.

We finished the bulletin board, but pretended to still be adding the final touches when Ascension passed us, escorting Craig Dockery and his mother, who'd been summoned to take him home early. She was smaller than Craig and wore an old flower-print dress, sharply ironed and starched. She walked like an example of good posture, staring straight ahead. Craig swung his shoulders and puffed his chest, but looked at the floor as he passed.

Rusty flipped a bird at their backs. We talked. We invented tortures for Craig that made us feel better, revenged.

"Snip his eyelids off and drip Tabasco sauce in his eyes," Rusty said.

"Tie him down," Wade suggested, "stick his pecker inside a loaf of bread, and release about five-hundred hungry ducks at him."

Joey even laughed a little.

I said, "Is anybody going with Donny Flynn's sister that you know of?"

"Why?" asked Rusty. "You think you're gonna get somethin off her?" They were all looking at me. I felt red come into my face.

"I just wondered if she liked anybody. She seems okay."

"She's strange. She tried to croak herself not long ago. Besides, she's too good-lookin for you." Rusty had three sisters and wasn't at all afraid of girls.

Wade said, "I kissed her at the Christmas bazaar two years ago."

"Wow," Rusty jeered. "What was she then, eight years old?"

"Ten-and-a-half. She used her tongue."

"Bullshit," I said, instantly sick and jealous.

"Don't believe me then."

"Tongue," Rusty said. "Wow. Put a goldfish in your mouth, you get the same feeling."

When the final bell rang (I was prepared for it this time), Margie went by with the others. She pressed a folded paper into my hand, looked at me, and walked away. The note said PLEASE CALL ME 394-7626—MARGIE.

"You lucky swine," said Tim, then he spit gloriously out over the railing and barely missed the tar wall.

The teachers lined up along the bulletin board and praised the artistry, worried over the violence. But I stopped hearing them.

It occurred to me then why the heart is always associated with love. Mine was a cannon. I had only to think of Margie, or see her, to start a barrage. And the touch of her hand and the words she'd given me made darkness close all around like when you dive into a river, and then it lightened and I surfaced standing in the hallway and listened to the boom, boom, boom of the universe.

A Discipline Problem

Every afternoon I walked my youngest brother home past Margie's house. Today I poked, watching for her, stopped to loosen and retie my shoelaces, and stopped again to shift my pack to the other shoulder. Peter, my brother, wandered on ahead, glancing back suspiciously over the hump of his green bookbag.

Margie's house took up the corner. Like the other houses on Victory Drive, it featured a front porch that could swallow my whole living room. Mr. Flynn, her daddy, had a construction company and nine children.

One of the Flynn boys was dribbling a basketball and whooshing it through a thrumming hoop on the side of their carport. I knew I ought to ring the bell and ask for Margie, but I dreaded the question in her family's faces. I would call her when I got home. I picked up a rock and slung it at a stop sign, missed, left.

†

Our house made me want to apologize. My mother went on about the charm of a carriage house, character, but it was the smallest house I'd ever seen, ivied brick squashed right up against the lane. The only advantage was the jumbo front yard, worthy of kickball, of boomerangs.

Tim and Rusty lived across the street in regular houses.

My brothers were feeding in front of the TV when I came in. Peter, the first-grader, was naked except for his uniform pants. He forked leftover potatoes out of a bowl and packed them into his cheeks, chewing steadily. Peter's arms and legs were thin, but his tummy was bulbed like an avocado.

John, the ten year old, was licking mayonnaise off a slice of white bread. He went to a special school and came home each day in a minibus. Many of his classmates were moon-faced with Chinese eyes, their ears and noses tiny. John's troubles were caused by not looking both ways when crossing a street three years earlier, an incident which sunk the family in debt and brought endless, petty miseries and embarrassments. John was also the only one of us who had black hair instead of brown.

"Did I get any mail?" I asked. I'd sent off for Sea Monkeys (The World's Only INSTANT LIVE PETS!).

They shook their heads no, hypnotized by *Bonanza* on our black-and-white TV. Little Joe and the bad guy were walloping each other's faces, each punch bomb-loud, on and on.

Spicy corned-beef steam wafted across from the kitchen. Mama had put a brisket on the stove between coming home from college and leaving for work, so it would be ready when Daddy arrived. I climbed the stairs, ducking to avoid the overhang.

Gretchen, our dachshund, was curled in the linen closet. She raised her head and patted her tail on the dirty laundry.

I shed my pack and my uniform and got into some corduroys and a T-shirt. I climbed up to my bunk and did my homework in an hour.

I popped some looseleaf from my binder and began a letter to Margie, but it got so corny I held a match to it until it was ashes, then flushed it.

The telephone in the hallway worried me. It might erupt at any moment with Margie's voice, or Father Kavanagh's.

I took *The Return of Tarzan* from my shelf and opened it to where I'd stuck a Baby Ruth wrapper. Trees heaved up in the room, unraveled vines in huge loops. Birds whistled. Roaring echoed off the ceiling. My muscles swelled and hardened, and I was the ape-man. To my Jane, I added tragic little wrist-scars. I jumped to the floor and smacked fists on my gorilla chest. I lifted the receiver and cleared my throat, but that only seemed to thicken whatever was in it. I stood and growled towards an acceptable voice. A drink of water worsened it. I decided to wait.

I trudged downstairs. My brothers were staring at the local news. Savannah's only black newsman stood on a downtown street talking to the camera while behind him a group of black people, mostly men, shouted some slogan. The younger men had bushy afros and were punching their fists overhead. The announcer said a black kid suspected of snatching a purse had been shot to death by a white policeman. A shaky scene of paramedics serving the body into an ambulance was followed by the pastor of the First African Primitive Baptist Church calling for a march through the city.

Peter crawled over and switched channels to *Green Acres*. Arnold the pig grunted at Mr. Ziffel. The television laughed.

Our front door opened, my mother arriving from the daycare center. "Peter, honey," she said, "lock up Mama's bike. She's got to fix your daddy's supper." Her keys hung in the lock, dangling a huge chain of beaded tassels which didn't prevent her from constantly losing them. She was the only mother I'd heard of who rode a bicycle.

From the kitchen, metal rang on metal, the familiar illusion that Mama was angry. If she was really angry, though, pots would be clanging off the walls. She had a demonic temper. She was a bad cook too. Most of her household attention went to the phone and the bathroom mirror.

28

Peter tramped into the kitchen to adore my mother and to set the table. Gretchen rocked downstairs with a prolonged clicking of toenails and stationed herself under the table. The phone rang—the illegal phone Daddy had wired into the kitchen—and Mama answered with a hello so sugary it sounded like a cartoon character. She began talking, laughing about a Statistics test. I relaxed, figuring she'd tie up the phone now with one of her admirers from school.

They visited on weekends. Mama would drop *American Pie* on the stereo and burn a cone of incense and they'd sit around. Professors' daughters who smelled like marijuana. A young man with girl's eyes and a piercing laugh. Men who got serious with Daddy about politics. A woman who drove a motorcycle. They'd sip martinis and grasshoppers and fog the room with cigarettes.

Mama passed the doorway with her ear pressed to the receiver, her shoulder raised to hold it, a cabbage in one hand and an onion in the other. I hated onions as much as it's possible to hate a vegetable.

Shortly, the Volkswagen putt-putted out front and my dad arrived. The mailbox creaked open as he checked to see if we'd missed something, then he creaked it shut to keep lizards and roaches out. His shoes whisked the mat. The screen door groaned open, keys jingled, Gretchen shot out from under the table barking for Daddy, for supper, jumping against the door, rattling it, tags clinking, and the lock snapped around and the door swung in.

"Gretchen! Get down! Here now." He pointed his toe to keep the dog off his clothes. His jacket was folded over his arm.

Daddy brought the stink of dead chickens inside. He was an accountant for a poultry distributor and had to tally thousands of dead birds each day.

"Howdy," he said, and he flipped on the lamp so the TV wouldn't ruin our eyes. He went to the kitchen, kissed my mother's cheek.

"Hello, lamb," she said, turning, winding herself in the phone cord, then laughing into the mouthpiece, "Oh no, not you! Bob just walked in. Mmm hmm." A fork clicked on a pot. The refrigerator peeled open, sucked shut, and a beer can cracked.

Daddy stepped into the doorway. "Everybody do okay in school today?" He cranked his tie loose and sipped some Old Milwaukee. "What'd you learn today, Peter?"

"About mammals," Peter said from behind him, near Mama.

"Great. John?"

John smiled painfully and looked around for clues. "Uhh . . ."

"Did you work on your reading?"

"Yeah. We read *Cat in the Hat* and stuff."

"Fantastic." Daddy sipped more beer. "What about you, Francis? Or are you too grown up now to learn anything?"

He was making me out to be a teenager again. "We drew a bulletin board all day. I didn't learn anything," I said obligingly.

My mother bye-byed and hung up the phone. She wrapped her arms around Daddy's neck and kissed him again, wrinkling her nose at the chicken smell.

He leaned his head back and said, "Kitchen smells good."

"Corned beef and cabbage," Mama said, then quickly, "on special this week." Of course she'd peeled off the price sticker when she came from the market Saturday. Also the stickers on the artichoke hearts and smoked salmon. ("Where the hell does the money go to?" Daddy had to ask at each month's end.)

To others, my parents must have seemed like they'd just stepped off the top of a wedding cake. Daddy was handsome, thin as a razor, dependable. Mama was pretty, sociable, pretentious. They were publicly affectionate. Both came from broken homes, so they were determined to endure their own marriage. They only argued over money, and had matching, savage tempers, but they directed them at us, never at each other.

"Petey," Dad said, "let's go put a shirt and shoes on, son. This ain't Africa."

They climbed the stairs. Daddy came down wearing a T-shirt and dingy bluejeans, stretched out at the knees. The poultry smell was tolerable now. Peter returned, civilized.

Mama and Daddy exchanged days. I watched TV.

"The taxes are a mess," Daddy said. He sipped beer at the kitchen table. "I've got a pile of paper this high. I laid awake all night worrying about it."

"I've got to cram for Statistics," Mama said. She sat down at the table. "And all the babies at work have chicken pox. It reminded me of when the boys were tiny."

Peter, raised above the rank of baby, smirked.

"Carlos is at it again," Dad said. "He planted a quail carcass in the secretary's desk. If he weren't Mr. Hamm's pet he'd be begging on the streets by now."

Something sizzled urgently.

"What's burning?" Daddy asked.

"Oh shit!" Mama jumped to the stove and blistered her finger flipping a lid off. She dashed a cup of water into the pot and prodded inside with a wooden spoon. She told us to wash up.

We sat around the little table and my mother dropped a knitted potholder in the center and placed the pot on it. Daddy said grace, then he worked knife and fork inside the pot and slid a wedge of cabbage and some meat onto each of our proffered plates. The dog squirmed between my feet.

Slivers of onion stuck to all the food, and the meat was scorched on one side. I scraped off all the onions I could and sculpted them into a little pyramid at the edge of my plate. Daddy watched me. He chewed slowly, the muscles at his temples pulsing.

"Eat up, son, that's good food."

I nibbled. It tasted like burnt onions with some beef flavor added.

"Francis must be thinking about his girlfriend," Mama said. "It's difficult to eat when you're in love, isn't it?"

31

The meat went down my throat like a golf ball. Girlfriends had never been mentioned before. My dad never, ever talked about women or sex, except for one antiseptic lecture when I was twelve. It was part of their big secret and accounted for years of whispering and locked doors. More recently I'd discovered a hidden spermicide applicator, some frilly, useless underwear, and a copy of *The Sensuous Woman* tucked between mattress and box springs. I didn't want to be included in this.

"I don't have a girlfriend."

My mother smiled. "The little Flynn girl seemed quite taken with you at church yesterday."

Peter and John looked at me funny. Dad chewed.

"It's none of your business," I said. Dad's eyes swung to me. I cut another piece of meat and chewed it.

"I just think it's cute," she said, and my ears stung. "You two would be sweet together."

With my mouth full, I snapped, "Would it be cute if I watched through y'all's keyhole during one of your 'discussions'? We could talk about that at dinner."

"Francis!" she gasped, faintly smiling.

"That's enough of that talk, mister." A speared chunk of meat was poised at Dad's chin. "Eat your supper."

"It's crawling with onions."

"That's perfectly good food, mister. This ain't a cafeteria. You eat what we have."

My mother sucked her burnt fingertip. She said, "Pick them off, Francis. I can't cook just for your tastes."

"I'm not eating this charred crap!" I shouted, dropping my fork in the plate and spitting out mangled meat.

"Apologize to your mother," my dad growled, slow and scary, a voice he must've learned in the Air Force. His teeth were clenched. He began to tremble. "Apologize or I'll tan your hide!"

Something gave way in me, like the weightlessness of sliding off the edge of a roof. I slapped the table, the plates jumped, and I hollered, "No!"

My father bolted up, his chair scraping back and slamming the wall, and he shakingly unbuckled his belt.

The belt was thick, black, and stamped with a series of horse heads. A relic from when he hosted cowboy movies at the TV station. He had quit when my mother got pregnant with me, because back then TV was new and didn't pay him enough to feed a whole family.

He yanked the chrome and turquoise buckle and the belt fluttered slapping through the loops, a familiar sound, but paralyzing like the rattle of a snake.

Mama said his name, touched his arm, and turned to me, perplexed.

The dog slithered out from under the table and floundered up the steps.

My father, a caricature of shuddering rage, stepped over and grabbed me by the arm. My brothers bowed their heads and peeked up from underneath, careful not to get implicated.

"Stand up there, boy!" He pulled me to my feet and swung the belt back up over his shoulder, then slashed it across my legs and whipped it backhanded across my butt. Back and forth, teeth gritted, eyes crazy, whipping, burning, his left hand locked on my arm like a trap. The belt buzzed through air, slapped, buzzed. Slapped. I lifted one leg, then the other, in a kind of reflexive jig.

There was a way to take it. You hold your arm a little ways from your body so the belt catches your wrist and wraps around it. There's a painless slap. You can catch about half the strokes that way. You only have to break into tears when you want him to stop.

I couldn't make myself cry.

I fell just outside the kitchen doorway. I curled onto the floor and my father turned me, distributing the stripes like basting a turkey. Silhouetted in the light of the doorway, my mother was screaming.

My father slashed and slashed me. I rolled. My brothers sat terrified. *The Beverly Hillbillies* was on TV. My mother pushed herself in front of my father and caught his arms and shrieked, "Bob! Jesus Christ you'll kill him!"

He stopped and stood over me, trembling, dangling the belt. His hair was wild. "Sometimes you just don't want to stop . . ." he said, and his eyes looked drugged, dazed, the way I felt.

"I suppose you've convinced him to eat his dinner now," Mama said angrily. Her anger baffled me, since she seemed to have been the catalyst.

Daddy fed the belt back through the loops. They sat.

On the living room floor I rolled up my flared pantslegs. There were the usual stripes, some bleeding welts. Mama winced. John and Peter paled like they'd taken the beating. For a moment I wished he had ruptured an artery so I could bleed to death in quiet reproach. The hernia ached.

Daddy said, "I guess you think you're some kind of man, not crying." He made a spitting sound.

My mother walked past me to the bathroom and returned with a tube of antiseptic. She squeezed out creamy worms and rubbed them into the welts. I tried not to flinch. Then I limped to the table (imitating gunshot heroes) and lowered myself into my chair, the way a yogi might sit on broken glass, or nails, well observed. Peter, the baby, squeezed little tears out of the corners of his eyes.

I ate the pile of onions first. They made me want to gag, so I held my breath and swallowed without chewing. Daddy looked at me, then quickly away, as if he'd just remembered why I was wolfing onions.

John pouted at his cabbage. "Why'd you hit him so much?" he asked, tactless as a four year old.

"Mind your own P's and Q's or you'll get a taste of it."

Mama said, "Your father's been having a difficult time at work." Daddy jabbed a square of meat into his mouth and ate reflectively.

"He'll be having difficulties at home, too, if he doesn't watch it." Daddy swallowed, cleared his throat. "Francis, I look forward to the day you have children of your own. I hope they drive you as crazy as y'all have driven me."

After dinner Mama told Peter and John to do the dishes instead of me, because I'd had a beating. I opened the front door.

"Hold on there, mister, where do you think you're going?" Daddy was sitting in front of the TV, picking his teeth.

"Tim's," I said. Actually I was thinking of stealing a drink somewhere and then going to see Margie Flynn, or maybe just walking to the lumberyard and jumping a freight train, good-bye troubles.

"You stay in tonight. This ain't a boardinghouse where you drop by to eat and sleep. Besides, the colored folks are all stirred up over that shooting. Probably be a riot."

"Fine," I sneered. "I'll just hang around so you can enjoy my company."

He sucked his teeth as if he was occupied, hadn't heard.

I got a glass in the kitchen and stretched to the top shelf of the pantry for his bottle of Jack Daniels. My brothers averted their eyes. I poured myself a glassfull and set the bottle back. I added ice cubes and stepped into the living room.

"Even the iced tea tastes like onions to me now." I took a big fiery swallow of whiskey right in front of my parents. My eyes watered. Daddy probed his teeth with the toothpick and made little bird noises.

The phone rang, I didn't care, and Mama sweetened up again.

I took my whiskey to the bathroom and drank fast. I shook my head and the whole bathroom shook around me. My face was strange in the mirror, didn't seem to have anything to do with me. The back of the toilet was stacked with cosmetics and hair curlers, spiky pink.

I rinsed the glass and brushed my teeth, twice. Combed my hair. Tucked my shirt in. All the details adults forget about which telegraph their drunkenness. The burn in my legs was fading.

I took my glass to the kitchen for my brothers to wash. Daddy was watching the network news. He burped and said, "Pardon me."

"Do you mind if I sit on the bench for a few minutes?" I asked. The effects of whiskey are better appreciated outside, where the entire world is transformed.

"It's getting dark. Don't stay out there long."

I enjoyed the shagginess of the grass. The stone bench seemed to dip and rise, raftlike. A swirl of swallows flickered in the gray between treetops, then spilled away. The moon was brightening, some stars beamed.

I lost the anger at my father. I even felt superior, a kind of martyr to his childish fury. He didn't whip me as often now as he had when I was little, but it had gotten more vigorous. I suppose he thought I might hit him back. But that would upset the world in some terrible way, so I never considered it.

A bat dipped and fluttered crazily over the yard. I raised my hand fast and he swung past it. Suddenly I felt like crying because I wanted Margie Flynn so badly. It seemed to me she'd make up for all the rest.

I walked back to the house, trees and stars weaving above me.

36

The door to our bedroom was locked from inside. I smacked on the panel. I heard my brothers opening and shutting drawers. I whacked the door again and again and yelled for them to open up. I was in a bad mood, and drunk.

Daddy thumped upstairs and said, "Don't bang on that door, son, you boys have already cracked it. Who'll pay for a new door?" His voice was more whiny than mean now.

"They're into my stuff again."

"You're lucky to have any stuff. You boys ruined all my things ages ago. I can't keep nothin around here." He leaned his ear to the door and rapped, large-knuckled, three short authoritative cracks as from a tack hammer. "Open this door, boys," and then in the Air Force voice, "I'm counting to three and if this door doesn't open, y'all are going to get it. One . . ."

No matter that he couldn't have whipped them through a locked door. It clicked open and John peered out guiltily. Peter dangled his legs from his bunk, casually peeling a scab from his elbow. One of my comic books jutted from the corner of a drawer, squashed. I kept my comics in mint condition. My art collection of sorts.

I charged over and unpinned the comic, started reorganizing. "Why don't you at least keep them neat?" I asked. "That way I wouldn't find out and I wouldn't get you back."

"There won't be anybody getting anybody back," Daddy proclaimed. "These are your brothers. John, Peter, if Francis is so selfish he won't share with you, then you have to play with your own toys." He walked to the stairway and glanced back. "Now, I mean it."

His steps moved off into the living room. I looked at my damaged comic. It was an old *Vault of Horror* from the 1950s, a treasure I paid thirty dollars for back when I had the paper route. The cover was torn now, the whole thing rippled like an accordion.

I grabbed John's throat and his hands jumped up and caught my wrists. I didn't squeeze. I knew I was drunk and stupid. I let go of him. Where my hand had been was an old scar, a small pink fold of skin where the doctors had opened his windpipe after the accident.

I tore the comic in half, crumpled it, and jammed it down in the wastebasket, surprised at how good that felt. This terrified my brothers. "Next time," I said, "ask first."

What Happened
to God

We vaguely said the Lord's Prayer and pledged allegiance to the flag, opened English books and raised hands and feared Sister Rosaria. Margie Flynn was in my head like a bad cold, blurring everything. It was a new kind of loneliness, a hurt I couldn't stop picking at.

I saw her brother Donny plastered into his latest broken arm, sowing thumbtacks into Joey O'Connor's seat when Joey went up to collect his spelling test. Joey was fat. He sat down hard and wrenched up with five silvery disks stuck to his bottom. He plucked out each tack and dropped it into his breast pocket and glowered through his glasses at Donny, like he was saving those tacks for revenge.

Tim was slumped in his seat, hungover apparently, drawing. He never studied. His dad was a college history professor. The Sullivans' house contained so many books and paintings I didn't know what the walls looked like.

At eleven, the class lined up according to height, Tim humiliated at the front of the boys' line, Wade towering proudly in the back. We collected our bag lunches and marched downstairs with the other half of the eighth grade.

We stood on the sidewalk. The caution-yellow school bus

waited at the curb, BLUEBIRD chromed into the grille. It was a new bus, and you could smell the fresh rubber. Mr. Thomas sat in the driver's seat and sipped orange juice from a squat carton. Mr. Thomas was also the janitor and handyman and had six children on scholarships at Blessed Heart.

Mrs. Barnes, our other eighth-grade teacher, stood beside the door. A honeybee was threatening her hairdo. She avoided it with casual little nods, because she was a science teacher. Her eyeglasses blazed. They always held light so you couldn't tell if she was watching you. Marty's mother was talking to her. Sister Rosaria moved down our line collecting permission slips, in case anyone got mauled. Some of the boys had forgotten to get them signed, but we fixed them up with forgeries at a quarter apiece.

Rosaria tucked the slips into a folder and waddled up to the bus. "I expect maturity from every one of you this afternoon," she said, small and frowning, beaked nose, a scallop of gray hair squashed where the veil sat. Mrs. Barnes said, "Let's go, people," and herded us in. Mr. Thomas winked and held his palm up as if expecting a fare. Tim slapped his hand, giving five the way the black kids did, then the four black boys did it, and at the end everybody was slapping Mr. Thomas's hand, a sound like slow applause.

Sister Ascension, our principal, climbed inside and heaved herself onto the seat beside Rosaria, who was a dwarf in comparison. The cushion flattened, sighing. She smiled all around, thick-lipped and cheerful.

I sat next to Tim, behind Wade and Rusty. The bus hummed and its brakes hissed and we began to roll. Tim moaned. He was paler than usual and his slicked-back hair was dull and stuck out in spikes as if to prove he felt bad. The skin under each eye was like a frog's throat.

"I guess you got drunk last night too," I said.

"Genius," Tim said. He spat yellow gunk out the window. He rustled a can of Coke from his lunch bag. He'd frozen it the night before so it would stay cold for lunch. The top and bottom of the can were swollen, and the seams were unfolding. Tim put his mouth over the outline of the tab hole. He lifted the tab and a burst of gassy slush exploded into his mouth. He choked. Caramel-colored mush ran out his nose. He gulped, opened his mouth, and leaned forward, a move I'd seen him make over toilets and sinks, and I swung my feet out of the way.

"I'm only trying to burp," he said. "After thirteen years of drinking sodas, you'd think I'd know how. My throat muscles won't coordinate." Tim leaned back and sucked at the cola slush. He patted a rectangular flatness in his lap, beneath the green uniform pants. "I've got another interesting 'bladder infection.'"

"What is it this time?" Last week he'd smuggled in *Lady Chatterley's Lover*. He'd been suspended once for bringing *The Communist Manifesto*.

"Poetry," Tim said from the corner of his mouth, gangster style. Rusty turned around in the seat in front of us. "William Blake. *The Marriage of Heaven and Hell*. Dangerous stuff."

Rusty dangled his arms over the back of the seat. "Right. Like they're gonna burn you at the stake for readin poetry."

"This guy raises your consciousness higher than most people can handle. It could give you a stroke, Russell."

"Hit me with a couple lines. I'm tough."

Tim glanced at the teachers, pulled the book out of his pants. "Blake was a prophet. He drew these pictures too."

"Just looks like a book to me," Rusty said.

"Yeah, well the Bible's just a book too."

Wade said, "The Bible's thicker."

"Listen to this. 'You never know what is enough unless you know what is more than enough.'" For us, Tim explained this in terms of drinking, though I more or less understood anyway.

"Okay," Rusty said. "That's not bad."

"That's nothing, here—" and we leaned in toward Tim. The book's cover swarmed with naked couples embracing, flying

41

together, and there were gaunt bending trees and a flock of birds, earth, air, fire, and water all swirling together at the bottom where a naked figure lay on a wave of fire, kissing another figure who floated on a fire-brightened cloud. The title blended organically with the picture. Tim said the original was painted in watercolor mixed with gold dust.

Tim quietly read a passage that said ancient poets had created gods to represent earthly places and things, and that later the priests had tricked people into forgetting the gods were symbols. " 'Thus men forgot that all deities reside in the human breast.' See? It's been twisted around so authority can use it on us like a bullwhip. Think about those Nazi evangelists on TV. The Crusades. The Inquisition. Galileo rotting in prison cause he said the earth moved around the sun . . ."

Every day, Tim Sullivan burned down the world, and then you lived in the places that withstood it, the ones that were strong to begin with. You loved this. You discovered that you could think too.

"Let me see those pictures," said Rusty. Across the aisle, Joey O'Connor was listening. We were on Highway 80 now, crossing the bridge over the Worthington River. The ground dropped away and became water, then rose up to meet us on the other side after an interval of shrimp boats.

The rest of the kids were in clumps of Go Fish, or flicking paper footballs, or singing "99 Bottles of Beer on the Wall." The teachers were being tolerant. The book had made us too quiet. Mrs. Barnes was turned towards us. Wedges of sky covered her eyes. She said, "Bring me whatever that is, Mr. Scalisi."

Rusty passed the book, the guilt, to Tim. Tim stared at him. Rusty shrugged. Tim swayed up to the front and presented the book to Mrs. Barnes as if it was a museum piece. Mr. Thomas watched in the big square mirror.

"Blake," Mrs. Barnes said, turning her eye mirrors on Tim. "A little advanced, I think, even for you."

"It's written simply enough for a six-year-old."

"So are the instructions for handguns." She flipped the pages and they cascaded in her lenses.

Sister Rosaria wagged her head at Tim, disappointed again. "You can pick this up after school," she said in her fluted nasal voice. "We'll have a literary discussion."

Tim sulked back, mouthing something. He sat behind Rusty and said, "Thanks, buddy."

The book was a cult relic now. Rusty had memorized a proverb and was repeating it like mantra: "The nakedness of woman is the work of God, the nakedness of woman . . ."

Tim said, "William Blake saw angels when he was a boy. He was really small, even after he grew up, but he once stood trial for beating up a soldier and throwing him out of his garden. Blake and his wife liked to sit naked in that garden and read from Genesis."

From across the aisle, Joey O'Connor said, "Jim Morrison named his band The Doors after something Blake wrote about cleansing the doors of perception." Joey collected records.

"Is that right?" Tim said. "Hey, I told you all Joey wasn't a moron." Tim's hangover dissolved in the enthusiasm for his hero. "Blake wrote the poetry, drew all the pictures, and even printed it himself. If he was alive now, I figure he'd be working for the comic books. That's what I'm going to do. Imagine a comic that would completely change the world, save it, like a new Bible."

"I thought y'all were supposed to be atheists or cubists or whatever." Joey twitched behind his glasses. His kinship to Sister Ascension, our principal, horrified him into occasional blasphemies of his own. "I mean, do you believe in God or what?"

"Not the name-brand God they serve here," Tim said. "That old guy with the beard, granting wishes out of the clouds to whoever says the most rosaries. That's bullshit. I believe in everything." Tim crossed his arms and sat back, a small king happy among eager faces. Even some of our ordinary classmates, the ones he labeled lemmings, were listening. "For me, the dog that pissed on the altar Sunday was as holy as anything else in this world. Holier."

The guys snickered.

"*God* is *dog* spelled backwards," Tim said, and his eyes flicked at me.

"Duh," Rusty said. "*Wow* spelled backwards is *wow*."

When Tim first appeared at Blessed Heart he had a strange accent and alien ideas. He read important books and had a chemistry set and knew the names of famous artists. I didn't know I was Southern until I saw what the North had done to him. He said he'd trade me what he knew and teach me how to draw if I'd teach him about the Georgia outdoors. I didn't know what the hell he meant. I was a generic residential kid, not backwoodsy, not even suburban.

He wanted me to guide him into the woods for some adventure. So, about three months into the sixth grade, we walked to Casey Canal to look for snakes. Tim was wearing a red-and-white-striped jersey like he'd seen on Pablo Picasso in photographs. We carried Kmart machetes in scabbards on our hips.

We floated an old door in the canal and called it a raft. It overturned. Tim dunked and his army cap spun on the surface. He broke water and snatched the cap and paddled to the shallows, spitting brown water. He fell onto the bank and lay there staring at me, dazed.

"I just learned to swim," he said. "This is a great day. I taught myself to swim."

"That was dog-paddling," I said, rather kindly. I peeled my shirt off and wrung it until water splattered. "It was instinct. You couldn't have kept that up for long."

"Hug a nut, Francis. I have never swam before in my life, and I just swam through water that was over my head." He shook his hair out and grinned. "It's true what my dad says, whatever doesn't kill you makes you stronger."

"Okay. So you swam." I wriggled back into the chilly shirt. My nipples were like BBs.

"The next deep part we get to, I'm going to swim all the way across to those woods. I don't have the slightest fear anymore."

We waded along for a while. Then Tim froze, cursed sharply, drew his machete, stared at the water.

"What?" I asked.

"Water moccasin!" He slashed the water around him. Some creature slid over my ankle. We slaughtered the water, laughing hysterically, and the water slowed the fat blades and turned them against us. I whacked my knee underwater. I heaved up on the bank, laughing, and Tim flopped beside me, and every root and fallen limb was a snake now. My knee leaked watery blood. My kneecap, though nicked and bruised, had kept the slice shallow.

"It was probably just a catfish or gar," I admitted. "It's kind of cold for moccasins."

"We'd better stay out of the water anyway, now," Tim said, pleased that real blood had entered into this. "We don't want to attract sharks."

"There aren't any sharks in canals," I said, thinking him big-city ignorant. The grass prickled the backs of my bare legs. The wound was hurting less. "This is fresh water, so-called."

"Yes, I know that, Huck Finn, but there've been freak shark attacks in fresh water. I can show you the books. Go ahead and take the chance if you want. You could get an infection too."

Anyway, I was cold. So we walked, poultry-skinned, our nipples beaded, teeth clicking.

"I'm starving," Tim said.

"Me too. But I don't have any money."

45

"Me neither. We could find a store and steal something."

This was new to me and seemed mortally dangerous. I dug my fists deep into my pockets.

"But we're wet and muddy and bleeding," Tim said. "Carrying weapons. They'd be suspicious."

We walked on, sneakers mushing, our breath beginning to trail in the November chill. We were in the black section now. Wooden houses swaybacked from decades of gravity, paint curling off like shavings. Wire and scrapwood fences held back the scruffy dogs. A rooster fluttered out from beneath a house and fluffed itself bigger at the fence, raising leg spurs at us. People called this Niggertown, the poorest neighborhood outside of the projects. We shouldn't have been there, but Tim was brave and naive, and this was part of my paper route.

"I'll get us some money," I said. "I can collect from some of my customers."

I tried six houses, fumbling with various crippled gates, before someone answered a door. A TV was flickering the window shades blue. The door peeked open, a vertical slice of black lady, two inches wide including an eye. She decided I wasn't a threat, and the door swung in to the extent of a chain latch, wide enough that I could've squeezed through. The woman's ankles bulged over the sides of her Keds, and her breasts were big as cabbages. Inside smelled something like dried sweat.

"I was afraid you was another Jehovah Witness," she said.

"No, ma'am. I'm just collecting for the *Morning News.*"

"You's early." Her eyes ran down me and she smiled, then tried to harden it. "Mercy, that's a big knife. You lookin to cut somebody?"

"No, ma'am. It's for moccasins. We were at Casey Canal."

"I don't tolerate no snakes around my place, no sir. My grandson cuts that grass every second week. I hope you killed some."

Tim was enjoying this from the sidewalk.

"Let me see do I have any money I can give you." She didn't

46

close the door or step back, but simply reached down into her blouse, and I suppose her brassiere, and extracted a balled handkerchief. She unrolled it. "You have to scuse an old lady. I was on my way to the bingo." She licked her finger, then unfolded a wad of bills and counted slowly.

"If you can't spare it, ma'am, that's all right." I remembered back to our old paperboy pestering my folks. I took a step backwards. "I'll just come back on the first."

"No, now, you've got some money comin. I know how y'all chirren need your spendin money. If y'all don't have none, you take it out your mama's pocketbook, ain't that right?" She narrowed her eyes into that suspicious, amused look women save for naughty boys. "I had six chirren of my own."

"You could just pay me half," I said. "We really only want to get a box of chicken or something."

"I see. That'll work out real nice." She counted three moist bills into my hand.

"Thank you, ma'am."

"Now don't forget to mark me down."

"Yes, ma'am."

"Mind you don't let no policeman see you carryin that knife, hear?" Her brow bunched. "You want me to get you a Band-Aid?"

"No, ma'am, thanks anyway." I had an idea the blood might prevent me from getting in trouble for being late.

"That's all right." She smiled, a front tooth outlined in gold. She closed the door a little, watched through it until I fastened her gate behind me. Her door clicked shut.

"Did I see her pull that money from under her tit?" Tim asked.

We followed the dirt road. I liked dirt roads in the summer. They seemed pleasant. But when it was chilly, like now, they seemed cruel somehow.

And then I saw the worst thing since my brother getting hit by a car. A dog limped beside the road, sniffing at trash cans. She was yellow, where the fur remained, raw gray in the patches taken over by mange. She held up one leg, the paw sideways, out-of-joint. One eye was a crust. Her swollen teats dragged in the dirt and her tail was curled in between her legs.

Tim's face drained so pale it scared me, like someone hemorrhaging.

I said, "I can't believe they let their animals suffer like that," requiring blame, wanting to say "niggers," but unable and knowing better, even back then.

Tim crept towards the dog with his hands opened as if to stroke her, chin quivering. The dog limped away, her one eye terrified white. Tim sobbed out a cloud of frost and screamed curses in every direction. He kicked a trash can until it buckled, then jumped on it, flattening it with a horrendous metal scraping. The dog hobbled farther away.

Light appeared at the corner of several curtains and shades. Across the street a big black kid stepped out onto a porch where the moths were already swirling at the light.

"You bet quit dat poundin fo I come make you quit." His accent was so extreme I could barely understand him and was sure Tim didn't. The boy held the screen door open, ready to go back inside as soon as his threat took.

Tim shrieked, "Whose dog is that?!" and I was afraid now because he didn't care what happened, his anger was so big.

"What dog?" the black kid said, stepping forward. The screen door whapped shut. "Ain't none a my dog. My dog inside by the TV. I was a little white boy, I'd be somewhere's else about now."

Tim hissed, crying, teeth bared, and ran to where the dog was crawling through garbage. He slipped his machete from its sheath and reared back with it.

I squeezed my eyes shut, but the slap of the blade, or whatever I heard, would return to me in fevers, in anxious half-dreams, and at moments when I thought I was happy. The dog never made a sound.

"What you wanna do that for, motherfucker?" The black boy's

sneakers smacked dirt coming towards us, and we both ran, machetes slapping our flanks, ran until the road became paved and
there were plenty of streetlights.

Tim stopped under a light, leaned back against the post, and
smacked his fists on his forehead, sliding down into a squat,
gagging on tears. He stood up and streaked dirty palms across
his cheeks and looked at me as if I was part of all this.

"There's no God, Francis, I hope you realize that. I'm not
ashamed for crying." One of his legs was dashed with blood. He
was shaking. He told me he'd never killed anything more than a
mosquito. "I would've like to cure that dog," he whispered, eyes
red, "but it was past that. There was no reason for it to be alive
except to suffer. Explain that."

We didn't spend my three dollars. I went to bed numb and
exhausted and plunged into sleep. I dreamed about it. I woke in
the darkness and God wasn't there anymore.

Where the
Wild Things Are

The highway had marsh on each side now. Egrets snaked their necks down and plucked minnows and fiddler crabs out of a creek. The bus crossed the bridge toward Marshland Island, half wrapped in a fence that wound among oaks and pines. Our bus passed through the gate and rumbled down a dirt road.

Mr. Thomas parked in a field between a rusty water tower and an old plantation house with brick wings added on. The effect was of a mansion with school buildings attached. Everywhere was green or striving toward green, and you smelled river mud and pine and salt water.

The teachers led us off the bus and packed us together on the field. Sister Ascension, the principal, plodded towards the building to find our guide. She climbed each step by raising one foot onto it, then bringing the other up alongside, like a toddler.

The traffic was a distant swish. I saw an osprey drifting in slow circles over the deeper part of the island, near the river.

"I wish I had my .22," said Pete Hancock. Pete was one of those kids whose lips move when they're reading.

"If it weren't for their claws," said Sister Rosaria, hand at her brow above the vulture nose, "I'd say they were God's best creatures."

Ascension came down the steps, her upper arms shuddering at each new level. Behind her was a tall guy in a flannel shirt. The nun, flushed from the effort of descending, said something and spread her rubbery lips in a smile, and the man faked a good-natured laugh, tilting his head back and squinting into the sun. He had a shaggy beard and mustache, brownish, and his hair was tied back in a ponytail. He wore little round glasses, hiking boots.

Mrs. Barnes clapped twice and said, "Listen up, people," and fixed an expectant smile. She turned to Ascension, and we turned too.

"Class," Ascension's voice was round and hollow, "this is Paul Steatham. He's a naturalist. He'll be showing us around and teaching us about the plants and animals on the island."

Paul Steatham petted his beard and smiled, eyes glittering.

Rusty mumbled, "That guy's smoked a few joints in his life."

His mother, right behind us, said, "Russell Scalisi, if you embarrass me in front of these teachers, I'll sell the television."

Paul, with the beard, explained that the animals on the island were originally native to Georgia. He spoke of extinction as if it was a clattering machine that might someday crush our own fingers. Because his voice was deep and rich, an axe thunking a tree stump, everyone listened. He asked us to stay on the trails and be quiet and not to tease the animals.

"These creatures aren't completely wild," he said, "because we feed them and they're used to seeing people. But they aren't pets. Some may eventually be released into the wild. They can be dangerous, okay? Now who's got a question?" He set his hands on his hips.

Eric Johnson, who was going to be a doctor like his father, raised his hand up stiff.

"Yessir," Paul said.

"What are the animals here used for?"

Paul pinched his beard and stroked it. "Nothing. They're not much use to us in our technological world. On the other hand, we're not much use to them either." His eyes crinkled at Eric, and his voice mellowed. "That was a good question, man. This island is just sort of an ark, I guess."

Ascension beamed. "It's our duty to preserve and protect God's creatures." Paul nodded.

Tim grabbed Rusty's shoulder and stood on tiptoe. "Do these animals of yours have souls? We're taught that they don't. Do you believe that?"

Sister Rosaria turned. She had on her harlequin glasses now. Her beakish nose pointed at Tim.

The man rolled his head and showed his bristly throat and chuckled in polite embarrassment. "I can't answer that one. Depends on your point of view. A Native American would say they have souls. I do know they're incapable of sin. Even when an animal kills, it's in innocence. Maybe they don't need souls." His eyes slid towards the teachers. He grinned. They smiled back, relaxed and charmed, except for Rosaria, who had reddened. She was coming our way.

"He's one of us," Tim said.

Rosaria pinched Tim's earlobe from behind, yanking it down so hard Tim smacked to his knees, and I wondered if she'd seen our awful comic book. The nun's teeth clenched, coffee-stained.

"Mr. Sullivan," she said, "you just stay beside me today. Any more cleverness and you will not graduate. Do you understand?" She jerked the earlobe for emphasis.

Tim stood up but kept his head cocked to ease the pull. He looked at Mrs. Barnes. She opposed physical punishment. Mrs. Barnes diverted her glance to Rusty's mother, who was frowning at us.

"You're a very small boy," said Rosaria, who was very small herself. She released the ear with a tug. "You'll probably be tiny all your life. You should compensate with intelligence and generosity, not rebellion and clownishness."

Tim hated himself for being small. He hung from the monkey bars for fifteen minutes every day, to stretch himself. Even a friendly mention of his height made him rabid. I knew he would get himself suspended now. I waited for the fireball of four-letter words. It was conceivable that he'd slap her face. But he only said, "Yes, Sister, I'm sorry. I was showing off." He swallowed hard.

She said something only he could hear and smirked kindly. Tim was even smaller now, a drooping of the shoulders, downcast eyes. As we walked along, he gradually drifted away from her, and Rosaria fell in with the teachers at the back. Tim was quiet beside me.

Paul guided us into the trees. Dead branches laid end to end marked the sides of the trail. We passed a pool of water, the surface solid with mulchy leaves and a dusting of new pollen. Frogs chirped and plunked in before we saw them. Melissa Anderson tightened a bow in her hair and asked if there were any snakes around.

Charles Sapp, our class reptile expert, sneered, "No, snakes only live in storybooks, Melissa."

Therese Parker, the girl with the pet raccoon, smiled adoringly.

Paul said, "Yes, please don't bother the snakes, girls."

Twigs and leaves crunched underfoot. I imagined I was an Indian and tried to walk silently, but couldn't. The trail ran under pines and mossy oaks and magnolias. Several of the boys found sticks to carry. The teachers kept telling us to stay on the trail. The girls clumped together in the center and pretended to be frightened, except for Therese Parker, who kept squatting at the edges to cluck at squirrels.

Birds squawked down at us or crackled through the dead leaves. The dullest of them, the mockingbirds, whistled and chirped and trilled as if they were trying to make us believe there were hundreds of them.

Sister Ascension walked at the front with Paul, her bulk filling the trail by half. Paul took slow steps to stay beside her. The breeze lifted her powder-blue veil, exposing the hair on the back of her head. At the rear, the teachers and Mrs. Scalisi all said how pretty it was, smiling up at the treetops, taking greedy breaths while diamonds of sunlight slid across their faces.

We crowded clattering onto a wooden bridge that spanned a marsh. Minnows flickered in the water holes. Rusty leaned out over the railing and turned his head from side to side. Suddenly he pointed right beneath the bridge. "There's an alligator!"

And then we could see it, a fat alligator basking at the edge of a water hole. The girls drew back to the other side of the bridge and clung to each other, tittering. The boys pressed against the rail, mouths open, clutching sticks. At the far end, a drainpipe splattered water out of an embankment. Charles Sapp calmly said, "There's another one," and aimed his finger at the marsh grass.

A huge gator, mud-gray, lay in the sun like a crusty statue. Near the drainpipe, behind him, a squirrel buzzed and fluffed its tail, and we wondered how many of them the gators got.

Paul began telling us about alligators, that they were related to the dinosaurs, to birds too, and like magic, like your eyes adjusting in a darkened room, a dozen of them materialized before us without any movement, sprawled in the mud, in the grass, or reduced to nostrils and eyes on the water's skin. Two orange and yellow babies, thin as snakes, slipped into the near pool. Paul made a soft oof-sound and cupped his hands around it, and the baby gators answered in the same voice. The girls moved closer for a peek.

Donny Flynn said the big ones looked rubber. He wanted proof they could move. He took some pennies from his pocket and cranked his arm back, enclosed in a plaster cast, but Mrs. Barnes said, "Don't you dare," before he could launch them.

Paul led us to a fence enclosing a stretch of pines and scrub. A little creek fed into a pool near the fence. As we stood there, five deer appeared. If you didn't concentrate, they vanished into the color of the woods, and you had to wait for the slow dip of a head, a flank twitching, before you could fit the outlines together again.

I pressed up to the fence. There was a blur of brown and tan and then the buck trotted over to me. He scraped his hooves on the ground beside the pond. He nodded and lowered the tines of his antlers through the chain-link and rasped them on metal, rolling his head. I put out my finger and touched the point of his antler, smooth, cool, and my heart hammered. The girls were cooing around me now, wanting to pet the deer.

Rusty and Tim crowded up beside me.

"I don't see how my dad can shoot those things," Rusty said. "Pretty neat, hunh?"

Tim said, "This is wild. I've got spring fever or something, man. I'd like to get ahold of a girl right now."

"There's about thirty of them right behind us," Rusty said.

"I mean girls I didn't know before they had breasts."

I'd known most of the girls since first grade, like sisters. But lately they had changed shape, they wore their uniforms differently, and even their voices had changed to fit the additional curves. The difference fascinated me, especially that moment with everything warming and sun-printed and greening, and part of what I felt for Margie touched them.

Paul rested a flanneled arm across the fencetop. "In a natural state, these deer would be preyed on. That keeps them fast and graceful, almost invisible, and prevents overpopulation. I'm sure you've studied that catastrophe. We're coming up on the predators next."

Rusty, Tim, Wade, and I lined up across the front and walked in step.

The trees dripped moss and sunlight. An occasional deerfly stung, was slapped against a neck, fell, and then rose buzzing to sting elsewhere. Our black uniform shoes gently thundered to a bend in the trail, then clapped up a long wooden plank onto a deck. A fence skirted the marsh in a wide oval and wires ran along it to a metal box mounted on a pole. I saw only trees and grass and the river beyond.

Past a green palmetto fan slid something brown. There were gasps, steps taken backwards or forwards. It was a large cat, a panther. The cat slunk by underneath us, its shoulder blades jabbing smoothly beneath the fur as it padded a worn path in the grass all the way around along the fence. The cat stopped and looked up. Its eyes flashed and held on Tim, who was leaning dangerously out over the log railing, his toes six inches off of the deck planks, his eyes bright as the panther's. My breath snagged as he tipped past his balance and flailed, treading air, but Rusty already had him by the belt, pulling him back before anyone else saw.

The cat dropped its gaze and prowled. Everyone crept closer. Paul, fallen behind with Ascension, crossed his arms, satisfied with our awe.

Tim whispered, "That animal saw something in me."

Rusty, whose mouth had been hanging open, said, "He saw eighty pounds of meat, is what."

Tim glowered. "Eighty-three."

Wade said, "I'm going to draw one of those. Look at its muscles."

I said nothing. Another cat, slightly smaller, appeared from the opposite side and began pacing towards the first one. The original cat raised its paw, fat as a mitten, and both panthers tensed and flattened and snarled at each other so that my eyes got wide. The panther swiped the air between them. The girls gasped, drew back again. Sticks were forgotten in the boys' hands as they stared at these animals that could surely kill them. It smelled like the scariest part of the circus.

"Mountain lions," Paul said quietly. "Cougars. Some folks up in the Appalachians call them 'painters' or panthers. They used to rule this part of the country, but there aren't many of them left."

"What happened to them?" asked Therese Parker, staring at

the cats, her hands twisting nervously into her plaid skirt so that it raised above her knees, showed gooseflesh you wanted to sink your teeth into.

"People killed them because they were dangerous, unpredictable. Now everything's safe." He smiled with one side of his mouth. "Automobiles and nuclear plants and all."

Craig Dockery, the kid who'd hurt the duck, asked which would win, a cougar or an African lion. Paul said it depended. Donny Flynn said his granddaddy had shot a cougar in Florida. Paul asked if he ate it, but Donny didn't know.

Tim nodded us over to the side away from the others.

Rusty said, "So how do we capture one of those things?"

"Blowgun," Tim said casually. "I bring my blowgun down here and tag the cat with an anesthetic dart."

"Where the hell we gonna get that stuff?"

"Steal it from a drugstore maybe. Or buy it off your sleazy drug buddy." Tim meant the orphan kid who visited Rusty's family one weekend a month.

"This is too risky," I said. "Joey was right."

"Risk leads to greatness," Tim said. "Your sweetheart will love it. Francis Doyle, lion hunter."

"We'd have to disconnect those wires," said Rusty. "This fence is electrified."

"So we'll bring wire-cutters and rubber gloves."

"Wait a minute," Rusty said. "How do we get the panther all the way from here to Blessed Heart? These son of a bitches weigh more than we do."

"We borrow a car," Tim said.

"Nuh, its gettin too complicated. Too many places we can mess up. We got to streamline it."

"Wade," Tim said, "if one of those cats was knocked out, could you carry it?"

Wade puffed his cheeks, weighing the cats, then exhaled. "Sure. No problem."

Rusty hissed. "That cat weighs a hundred and fifty pounds."

"I weigh almost that. I've been lifting weights. I can hold that much on my shoulders."

"Tim's talkin about carryin it eight miles to Blessed Heart in the middle of the night. Without attractin attention." Rusty shook his head and grimaced like he tasted something bad. "No way."

"We could walk through the woods," Wade said. "I could rest every once in a while. We could take turns."

"Not me," I said, relieved that it was seeming less possible. "Doctor's excuse, hernia."

Rusty shook his head again. "Tim couldn't lift it either."

"Fuck you," Tim said. "I could pull it in a wagon."

"Nuh," said Rusty. "It's just not . . . not—what's the word?"

"Feasible," said Tim. "But I'll make it feasible. I'm plugged in to this."

We followed Paul and the others to another deck. There was a giant live oak in the center of the area.

Paul said, "There's a bobcat up there, see?"

The limbs swayed in the breeze, moss waving, leaves rippling, and then part of a limb flowed down itself towards the trunk, flicked a short tail up, and became a cat. The trunk of the tree and the tops of the limbs were red-brown where claws had scoured the bark.

"These fellas still live in the woods all over the place," Paul said. "But you'd have to use dogs to find them."

The bobcat flowed back up the trunk, its stubby tail curled forward and swishing. It jumped to a higher limb and stuck quick on top like a magnet.

Tim called out, "Are they dangerous?"

Paul said, "Sure. They can kill full-grown deer. Pioneers thought they rode deer through the forests the way we ride horses. Actually, this is because they kill by jumping on the deer's back and biting through the spinal cord or jugular." Paul's fingers became jaws and he clamped them on his neck. The girls moaned. "If they don't succeed right away, they're in for one heck of a ride. Normally they won't prey on people, though there have been some rare attacks on children."

Tim was already gloating. "How much do they weigh?"

"Generally about twenty-five pounds. These lazy cats are a little plumper. There's another one in that bush to the right."

The new cat's eyes floated in the green and brown.

"I can picture a rope dangling from that tree limb," said Tim quietly. "I see us doping the wildcat and carrying it back in a pillowcase. On our bikes. Then we're out of school, out of trouble, and have something amazing to tell our grandchildren."

"That's just a chicken-wire fence," Rusty said. "No juice to fool with."

"What about it, Francis?" Tim asked.

My palms had moistened, because I could see us doing it. I was scared because I wasn't very scared. "Easy as pie."

"These cats don't look dangerous to me," said Wade. "I liked the big ones better."

"This is smarter, Wade. Stripped down. It reminds me of those Picasso drawings of the bull that got simpler and simpler until it was just a couple of lines. But you still saw the bull. You know the ones?"

That comparison sparked an idea in my own head. "You haven't got to the final step yet."

"What's that?" Tim asked.

"We don't take the cat to school at all. We just set it free. It's reported missing, we leave the notes and bust a window— maybe leave some bobcat droppings or something. And since they won't find the cat, it'll take them longer to decide to re-open school. We don't endanger students or the cat, so if we get caught, it's nothing."

Rusty said, "Doesn't that defeat the whole purpose? Hell, why not set the cougars free too?"

"No," Tim said. "They're too big to live in these woods. Hell,

I believe Francis is right. It'll be beautiful. It'll take a minimum of effort but'll accomplish the same thing."

The bobcat padded out to the end of a limb and cawed, almost like a bird. The girls made kissy noises and stretched their hands out as if to be licked. Melissa Anderson wished for a bowl of milk.

"Lemmings," Tim said. "Those cats would as soon rip their throats out."

"It does look pretty much like a house cat," Rusty said. "I don't believe it'll close the school down."

"It could kill a first-grader," Tim said. "Look at the size of those paws, the way it moves through that tree. It's an economy-size panther. It's got handfuls of razors. Run up your chest and swallow your throat."

Rusty said, "I say we train it to rip Rosaria's head off. That'll get us out of class."

Tim laughed, delighted at the absurdity and gore. Joey O'Connor wandered up beside him and cleared his throat with a grunt.

"All right," Joey said, as if finishing a prior conversation. "I'll help y'all nab the wildcat."

Tim said, "Forget it, Joey. We've given up on the plan and decided to just take the consequences."

Joey squinted, wiped his glasses on his shirt. "No, no. I think you ought to go through with it. Otherwise, we're doomed. I've worked this all out in my mind. I've started doing exercises."

"I don't know what you're talking about." Tim grinned at Rusty. Joey would be going with us.

I enjoyed the rest of the trail. I felt almost strong, being outside among animals. Paul showed us sleepy black bears and an otter that slicked through its pond like a fish and moved easy as a weasel on land. We saw wolves. Their den was in tree roots, but they ran around the pen constantly. I think they smelled the deer.

We watched pelicans eat. They scraped stiff fish from the concrete, slid them into their pouches with a slapping of their bills, then washed them down with a gulp of water. You saw the bulge travel down the neck. An eagle shrieked at us. I'd never heard that before. At the end, raw-headed vultures, a hawk, and a white owl watched us pass. The owl's head swiveled all the way around until it was backwards.

We walked to the bus for lunch. Mr. Thomas was asleep with his mouth open. We sat in the field and ate while Paul lectured on ecology and played an eight-track tape of music from India. The nuns' faces beaded with sweat because they wore the most clothes. At the end of the speech everybody clapped, cheered, and Paul smiled and told us to visit again.

This was the only field trip I'd been on that ended in a field. We had to pick up every bit of trash, even what wasn't ours. We got back on the bus. Joey laid thumbtacks in Donny's seat, but Melissa started to sit there and he had to stop her and remove them. Paul waved at us as we rolled away.

The back of my neck was tight with sunburn, and I found two ticks the size of pinheads on my arm. I popped them loose and flicked them out the window.

A Priest with
a Girlfriend

Everybody brought chicken legs to Science class. Brown paper lavatory towels were spread on all the desktops. Mrs. Barnes sent Melissa Anderson around with a box of one-sided razor blades, and we took one each. We followed along with Mrs. Barnes, slicing skin into pink muscle and peeling away tendons and silky ligaments and splitting the bones to find the squishy marrow. The classroom smelled like my dad. My hands got greasy. Eight kids cut their fingers and Mrs. Barnes sent Melissa around with a tin of Band-Aids.

In front of me, Donny Flynn used his razor to carve yet another swastika into the cast on his arm. Every desk he'd ever sat in was marked with a swastika. With equal ignorance, he wore a Confederate States of America belt buckle.

The razor blades made me think of his sister's wrist scars. I still lacked the nerve to call her.

Tim and Rusty dared each other into eating slivers of raw chicken. The class roared. Mrs. Barnes, her eyeglasses white with fluorescence, rapped the pointer on her desk and told them not to complain to her when they got salmonella.

We wrapped the drumsticks in the paper towels and dropped them in a plastic garbage bag up front. Mr. Thomas, the janitor, came in at the end and licked his lips archly and took the bag away.

At lunchtime we trooped downstairs to the cafeteria, into the oily crusty smell of, yes, fried chicken.

"Coincidence my ass," Rusty said. "These cheap bitches don't waste a thing."

We cut past all the seventh-graders in line and took plates of chicken and butter beans. It wasn't the dissected chicken, but I still didn't want it. So much trouble and change was occurring that my stomach had rebelled.

Tim had brought a coconut for lunch. He punched holes in the soft parts with a ball-point pen, then sucked out the milk through a straw. He cracked the shell open on the floor and peeled out pieces of white meat.

We huddled at the end of our table and talked about the Wild-cat Caper. Rusty, Tim, and Wade shared sly looks that made me think they had a secret from me. I only ate about half my chicken. My hands still smelled like the raw stuff. Tim gave me some coconut, and on the way out I bought SweeTarts at the candy window.

All of us walked to the corner and waited for the patrol boys to stop traffic, then crossed over to Daffin Park where we had our recesses. Wade and Rusty bounced a soccer ball between them. Tim drummed a ragged copy of Orwell's *Animal Farm* on his leg. We passed our old merry-go-round and the swings and the ladder tower, all of them made of smooth dirty pipe that smelled the way dimes taste.

On the other side was the community swimming pool, empty inside a locked fence, and beyond that the pond, its surface carpeted with green algae. White ducks, minus the injured one, drifted across in search of picnickers likely to fling bread.

Father O'Leary was waiting in the field already, a whistle dangling below his Roman collar. Rusty tossed the ball to him and he kept it in the air with little kicks.

The young priest coached us once a week now. Before that, we sometimes played a version of rugby whose only rule was you couldn't touch the ball with your fingers. The players obeyed this by carrying it in their fists, and you could do anything, even punch a kid in the mouth to get the ball from him.

Father O'Leary taught us soccer rules, sportsmanship, positions, the way they did it in Ireland. He talked about organizing a school soccer team.

I couldn't do all the running and kicking anymore because of the hernia. Tim sat out sometimes to keep me company and to read. He was always one of the last picked for a team anyway, because he was so small.

We sank down at the field's edge, on the roots of a giant oak. I could feel the little scabs on my legs pull, from the whipping. I munched my candy. The others scurried across the field, kicking the checkered ball, shouting. The seventh-grade boys gathered farther up, on the red clay of the softball diamond. Steven, Wade's younger brother and also the tallest in his class, tossed some poor kid's glove up and popped it into the outfield with an aluminum bat. He laughed wildly, slung the bat after it. Wade claimed their parents' divorce was responsible for this behavior. Behind the chain-link of the batting cage were some old bleachers where the girls were pairing up to gossip. Margie Flynn, I knew, sometimes stayed in the library after lunch.

Rusty hustled across the field, Wade beside him. Rusty kicked the ball along, ran after it, kicked again. Father O'Leary, on the other team, ran out to block him, the stringed whistle bouncing on his black shirtfront, and Rusty hooked the ball with his orthopedic shoe and it swished out sideways and Wade kicked it at the goal line. Donny Flynn flung himself vainly at the ball and thumped to the ground, plaster cast first. "Motherfucker!" he shouted.

Father O'Leary squinted towards the pond as if he hadn't heard. Donny raised up on his belly with a "so what?" sneer.

O'Leary was slight and dark with a droopy mustache like a

bandito. He had devilish pointed eyebrows and smiled a lot, but he was shy. I'd heard my mom whispering to Rusty's mom on the telephone that he had a girlfriend in the parish and might leave the priesthood. I hoped not. He was the nicest of our priests. He would've already forgiven us for *Sodom vs. Gomorrah* '74.

Donny fetched the ball and hurled it back. Way across, on the bleachers, a couple of girls had pulled yarn and needles out of shopping bags. Others were playing games in notebooks, Hangman probably. And there was Margie Flynn, sitting alone at the end, hands folded in her lap. I couldn't see her eyes at that distance.

Craig Dockery and the other black kids had boycotted soccer because of the purse-snatcher killing. I didn't see the connection. They clumped around the drinking fountain, playing a game where you put your palms on the other guy's palms and he tries to slap your hands before you can draw them away.

Tim had his exhausted paperback of *Animal Farm* open to a page of underlined sentences. He held a pen to his mouth and nibbled the cap. "So you think you're brave enough for the Wildcat Caper?" He didn't look up.

I said I reckoned I was stupid enough to do it.

"Good. Then you won't have any problem with this other rite of manhood I've arranged for you."

"Manhood?"

His eyes flicked up at me, then back to the page. "I sent her a note."

My heart contracted. "What, who?"

"A love note to Margie Flynn. I signed your name."

"Oh God! You're kidding, right?" I felt myself going red. I didn't dare look in her direction.

"I'm serious. You've got the kind of opportunity I'd sacrifice a finger for, and I'll be damned if I'll sit around while you let it evaporate, man." He took the pen from his mouth and underlined something. He looked at me.

I flung my head down into my hands. "Goddamn it, Tim, why

the hell did you do this to me? I'm too mortified to ever face her now, you asshole."

"It doesn't call for this much suffering, Francis. It was a few sentences designed to make her fall in love with you. I'm tired of seeing you mooning around and her looking like the end of the world. Besides, I bet Rusty five bucks you'd go steady."

Caustic ripples of shame rose up in me. I moaned. "What did it say?" I felt that all the girls were laughing at me across the park. I peeked through my fingers. They weren't all laughing.

"I told her—in your vocabulary—that you thought she was the most wonderful girl in the school but you didn't know how to tell her. I worked in a couple lines from Robert Frost. She's smart, she'll get it. Trust me." He was grinning like an imp, his long hair tucked behind his ears.

"Do you realize how goofy you've made me sound? I ought to beat your ass," I said.

"You can't. I'd kick you right in the hernia. Besides, it succeeded. Margie's been staring at you for ten minutes." He paused to let this work on me. "I told her how you really feel, didn't I?"

"Maybe so, but Jesus! I wanted to wait until I felt ready . . ."

"Exactly, Francine, but you never feel ready for anything. You never think you're good enough. So I did you a favor. I'm your good angel." He cuffed my shoulder and I shrugged violently. "She's sitting over there sighing, buddy. She's probably written your name on her notebook about a hundred times, and I bet she thinks about you when Neil Diamond songs play on the radio."

"You've made it sickening. You're like my mother."

"I'm realistic. She's twelve years old, man. She's not sophisticated enough to not like you. Sure she looks like she stepped out of a Frazetta painting, and she's nice, intelligent, but she's a kid. Even more than us. She's probably flattered out of her mind. Don't agonize, go take your damn bounty!"

"I believe I'll join the priesthood," I said miserably.

"Are you really mad at me?"

"Why should I be mad?" I told him he was a dick.

"Fuck you, then. Join the ranks of the lemmings. And when you have your hernia operation you might as well get them to snip your nuts off." He stared into his book.

I slid down between the thick oak roots and they rode up alongside me like railings. "Look," I said, "I know you're trying to give me a friendly push, but I like this girl too much. I feel like I'm going to faint when I get near her."

"So tell her that stuff, fruitbat, not me."

Fat Joey O'Connor fouled the soccer ball and it skidded towards us. I put out my foot and it bounced off my sole. Tim stood and slung it back at them.

I said, "Why don't you snare a girlfriend? You're always tricking other people into doing things."

He looked grim. "It won't happen for me. I'm this little stick figure with an enlarged brain or something. I have to do things through you guys."

"Bullshit. If you're such a genius, why don't you use that to impress girls?"

"I'm the size of a nine-year-old, if you hadn't noticed. Asshole. But I'm as smart as a grown-up. And even if I could tolerate a twelve-year-old girl, she's not going to be impressed by a brilliant midget."

"Somebody like Margie might."

"Well. You want me to experiment on her?"

"No . . . but there might be . . ."

"You go ahead. I'll see how it works for you first."

To avoid punching him, I shoved off the roots and walked away. "I'm not your goddamn guinea pig," I said, angry and shaking and ashamed.

"That's real noble," Tim called. "Puss out. If you were the Boy Scout you think you are, you'd walk right over and deal with her!"

I kept walking furiously. The soccer players shifted downfield.

I looked over and saw that Margie really was watching me, and I dropped my eyes. There were soft mounds of clover puffed through the grass. Someone shouted, "Heads up!" and the ball boinged off my shoulder and swished to the grass beside me and then a body fell on me from behind and my teeth snapped and I sprawled. Kevin Hurley, our athlete, stumbled over me and booted the ball away. He glared back like I was an idiot, shouting, "I said, 'Heads up.'" Kevin had terrycloth sweatbands on both wrists. The players stampeded around me. Rusty pounded past, laughing and wheezing.

I got to my knees and turned to the bleachers. Margie's hands were over her mouth. She'd seen me get tackled.

I walked straight towards her, my knees dark with grass stains. Margie kept looking away, then back at me, until she was sure I wasn't going to stop. Her legs were together, slanted sideways out of her skirt, white socks bunched at her ankles. She smoothed the green plaid over her thighs and folded her hands in her lap.

I shoved my fists in my pockets and stood right in front of her so the other girls wouldn't hear. Some of them were leaning in to each other now, whispering. I heard a thunk and glared over at the softball diamond where the ball was shrinking into the air and a boy was running the bases, a plume of orange dust rising from the clay at his heels.

"Look," I said, sounding much too angry, "I didn't send that note. An ex-friend of mine did it as a joke." I looked at her, felt ugly and stupid.

She said, "Oh," and stared at the ground with her lips slightly apart, wounded possibly.

I wanted to cry now. I turned completely around and watched the soccer game. Margie's brother Donny smacked Pat Doolan in the neck with his cast and O'Leary blew the whistle.

"I just wanted you to know I didn't write it," I said. I dug a heel into the new wispy grass and turned it, grinding. I glanced back at her. She nodded without looking at me, and her hands tightened in her lap.

"I didn't really think you wrote it," she said.

"Well, I didn't. See you around." I hunched my shoulders and walked away, hands in pockets, sick in love with her and furious now at myself. I whirled and stared. Margie brushed her hair back, twisting it over gold with a little turn of her hand, an awkward, innocent imitation of what a woman would do, and she looked very small and vulnerable and I wanted to hold her. I walked back to her.

I kept my eyes on her hands. "I'm real sorry, I mean if I sounded real mean just then," I bumbled. "I was only mad about the joke."

"It's okay. Thanks for being honest, Francis."

My name, softening out of her mouth, the magic little combination of teeth, lips, and tongue, stunned me like a cherry bomb did once, too near, the world exploding into clear, startling quiet. My attraction to her at that moment tugged so heavily I was actually leaning down towards her, and her least gesture became unbearably precious, the delicate closing of her mouth, her fingers relaxing in her lap, the sudden soothing green of her upturned eyes. Her awareness of me made the entire universe a shimmering drunken joy.

I told Margie that everything in the note was true. Blood bumped in my neck. "I think about you all the time," I said quickly. "It keeps me awake at night." I turned away and saw the priest butt the ball with his head. The ball fell, boys swarmed it. "I guess you must think that's pretty creepy."

Margie touched my arm and all the breath went out of me. Her thumb moved across my forearm. "I'm sleeping okay for the first time in months," she said, "and I dream about you. Your hands are wonderful." She laid her hand back in her lap and lowered her head, then looked up and smiled. "I mean, I think you're smart and nice."

"Same here," I said vacantly.

We tried not to look at each other for a minute, smiling each time we did. Except for the tiny scars on her wrists, she seemed perfect to me, and so I loved the scars, because they meant that I could save her from something, and save myself. When our eyes held, I wasn't there anymore, but I felt like I was looking in a strange mirror and recognizing myself. The air dazzled me. I breathed sunlight, and distances melted away and I stood there peacefully. There were faraway pleasant shouts, birds calling.

I stuffed myself with the details of her face, then the rest of her, the careless beautiful hair, thin girl's body, slick gorgeous ankles. A thrill climbed from my stomach and tingled up inside my ears.

I forced myself back into myself.

"Could I meet you in the circle park after dinner sometime?" I asked.

"I'd love to," she said. She turned her hands over, so the scars didn't show.

"What about tomorrow night?" I guessed that would give me time to get used to the situation.

"I'm already waiting."

Some part of me wanted to shout, whoop, and this in itself was shocking. I started backing away on loose legs. I couldn't take any more. I was insane for this girl.

"What's your middle name?" I called, retreating.

"Angela. What's yours?"

I hesitated, having trapped myself. "Duncan. I could change it."

"See you tomorrow night." She waved, the sprinkle of fingers, and a wonderful smile, all having to do with me. The other girls were looking too, but differently, as if I had on nice clothes or had grown tall. I put my fists in my pockets, figuring three bulges were less conspicuous than the one.

I turned around and smacked face-first into a metal fencepost. I saw sparkles, and the pain burned tears into my eyes. I felt a trickle of blood run out of my nose, wiped it, and knew it was smeared across my face. I turned back. Margie's hands were at her mouth again, and the other girls were giggling. One of them said something about true love that should've embarrassed me, and didn't.

I smiled at Margie, then turned back to the fencepost and deliberately thumped my forehead against the metal. It rang like a softball had struck it, but didn't hurt, because I used the hard part of my skull, the way O'Leary taught us in soccer. I felt like a boy pretending to be a boy, so I laughed at myself, felt another dribble of blood, and Margie laughed into her hands, wide-eyed, and I walked away, treading happy grass, and soon I was leaning back with tree bark rough against my shoulder blades.

Tim had his book turned down over one knee. "I didn't expect you to get your ass totally kicked talking to a girl."

"You're a horrible little bastard," I said. "Lucky for you, everything worked out okay."

"Delirious. You've taken three blows to the head in five minutes. I think you're a masochist. Hey . . ." He passed his hand back and forth in front of my face. "Snap out of it and thank your buddy."

I sniffled and tasted blood. The soccer players blurred past Margie. On the diamond, the softball teams were exchanging places, tossing gloves to the field team, and trailing small rounded shadows in the afternoon. I lifted my hand and Margie waved again. It seemed miraculous.

"You look like a junkie." Tim picked up his book again. "I hope you can shake the fairy dust out of your head for next weekend. We've got to get to that bobcat before you two can live happily ever after."

"Thanks," I said. Everything was nice. I spit on my hand and wiped the red off my face. It was warm, breezy, and the shadows of clouds chased bright green spaces along the field. My friend chuckled. I'd have to say I was happy. A priest with a girlfriend kicked the ball past the goalie and boys cheered. Solid against my back was the great oak, hundreds of years old, evergreen.

Did You Think
I Was Tame?

Prior to meeting Margie, I sat with my friends in Wade's house and heard their advice and attempted to drink away my fear. I held my breath and gulped silvery watered gin, listening to Elton John on the stereo, garbled and straining in a likable way, above his heartbroken piano. The music grew lovelier with each swallow, though one speaker was blown so that the bass parts were fuzzy. The alcohol rolled over me like a warm breathable wave that edged everything with light and made my friends friendlier. The songs were melancholy, and we grew deliberately, pleasantly depressed.

Wade's mother was out with her boyfriend. The house was furnished in imitation Spanish, woodgrained, polished, stuccoed. You smelled burnt hair and chemicals from the garage room where she ran a small beauty parlor. We'd already been pestered for drinking by Wade's little brother Steven, but we'd ordered him into his room. When threatened, he went.

Wade, sitting at the head of the dining room table, copied a panel from *Swamp Thing* onto a piece of white cardboard, his nose almost touching it as he worked. "Margie'll let you do whatever you want," he said.

I didn't want to hear that. I had never kissed a girl. When I was nine, though, I convinced Ann Doolan to slide her panties down for me. I dropped my pants as part of the deal. We touched each other in her garage. I remember a creased blankness which didn't do much for me. Somehow her daddy found out and called my folks, and my dad whipped me until I pretended to cry. Rusty told everybody she was my girlfriend, so I stopped talking to her.

Tim said, "I wish girls were as easy to get as booze."

"They are," Rusty said, leaning his chair back onto two legs. "You just don't know any."

"I know plenty of them."

"They don't know you. You've never even held hands with a girl. You could be a homo for all you know."

Tim said, "Thank you, Russell, I feel better now." He took a huge gulp of gin and fell to doing push-ups to speed it through his bloodstream. He wobbled up and draped himself across a chair in a miniature of decadence. "I'm a hero trapped in the body of a candyass."

The stereo needle rasped in the run-out grooves of the record, then the arm lifted, retreated, and dropped, and Elton started bawling it out again.

Wade blew on his drawing to dry the ink. He was outfitted in a tank top that featured his muscles and underarm hair. "I found something that feels like the real thing," he said in his he-man voice. He went on to confess a solitary act with a warm washcloth and soap, which made me uncomfortable in spite of the gin.

Rusty, who grew hard-boiled after enough drinks to make me pass out, said, "How do you think you know what the real thing feels like?"

"Well, I imagine that's what it's like. I fingered a girl once."

"Please tell me it wasn't Margie," I said.

"Wasn't Margie."

Rusty smacked his hand to his forehead. "He imagines! I can imagine I did it with Raquel Welch, but it's still bullshit."

"I've tried that beating-off crap," Tim said. "The only feeling I get is that my parents are watching me with secret cameras."

"You're not physically mature yet," said Wade, bass.

"So what? I'd just as soon skip all the rude hair and pimples, thanks. And just who the hell are all these females you guys have supposedly messed with?"

"I'm protecting the innocent," Rusty said. "Girls get p.o.'d if you tell, then they won't let you anymore. My sisters told me that."

"Just name two."

"Hand me that *Mad* magazine, will you, Rusty?" I said.

"I've never touched Margie Flynn either," he said. "So don't cry."

"I can't feel my lips," Wade said, and giggled. "You think Salvador Dali ever gets this wasted?"

Steven came out of his room, *Famous Monsters of Filmland* in hand, and said he was going to tell on Wade unless we let him drink with us.

✝

The gin still burned inside me with the shape of my gullet, but my heart was a squirrel's heart. I spat my gum out, began walking down the middle of the street. The sun gleamed through a bright green tunnel of trees and bushes. A single wide lawn unrolled from corner to corner of every block, squared into front yards by pink or white walls of azaleas. I passed Blessed Heart School, tried not to think about it. I tipped my head back, gazed up, and soon fooled myself that I was walking on the sky, staring down at stalagmites of moss.

At the center of the park I swung the world right-side-up again, and now that seemed strange too, and I liked it. I inhaled the spring smell of sweet gum, grass, honeysuckle, and felt suddenly older. Like someone with a camera, I was conscious of now turning straight into memory, the past.

The circle was half a block wide. I didn't see Margie. Then my name floated to me faintly, like the singing you begin to hear around creeks in the woods, and I revolved, the park swirled around me, a carousel, and wisps of pink and powder-blue blinked through the leaves of a giant magnolia trailing its lower limbs on the ground. The branches there opened and Margie Flynn stepped out, and the big waxy leaves snapped fluttering behind her.

The alcohol dizzied me then, poured through me. Carefully, I walked over, as strange as walking on the moon.

Margie tugged down the denim at her knee and a single wrinkle at her thigh vanished. Her sweater was soft and curvy, a bright layer of cotton candy. Out of uniform, almost as startling as naked.

"You've been waiting," I said. It sounded so stupid I wanted to smack myself.

"I couldn't eat dinner." Margie wrinkled her nose, freckles bunching. "My stomach felt sort of funny."

We stood there. I took my hands out of my pockets, looked up at the streetlamp, breathed, looked at Margie, buried my hands in my pockets, smiled. She smiled back at me. We stood there.

"Um," she said. "Want to walk around or something?"

We walked the edge of the circle. Margie said she'd heard about the duck, said we were brave to take up for it, and I wished I had been. Weeds fluttered against our pantslegs, and we stepped on clover, and I snuck looks at her, and squirrels buzzed and corkscrewed up trees as we passed.

"Your bulletin board was great," Margie said. "Sick, but great. You're really talented."

"I mostly just did the coloring. Tim Sullivan's the real artist, he taught the rest of us. But thanks."

"He's the one who sent me that note, right?"

"Right."

"He sure spits a lot."

"Sinus problems."

"I think he's trying to act tough because he's so small."

"That too, I reckon. He's smarter than the teachers, though."

"Are y'all in trouble with Kavanagh or something?"

I told her about *Sodom vs. Gomorrah '74,* and she laughed and said she'd heard about it, which firmed my suspicion that her brother Donny was the culprit who turned it in.

"Are y'all really atheists?"

She sounded maybe intrigued, so I said we were.

"Wow. I guess you don't believe in ghosts, then."

"I don't know. I haven't got it all worked out yet."

"Because I believe in them," she said. "My house is sort of haunted." She looked at me to see if I was taking this as a joke. Dozens of houses in Savannah are supposedly haunted. There are books on it. "I think maybe it's like film or records, stuff like that," she said, "that takes an imprint. Or even like those poor Japanese people whose shadows got burned into the walls by the atom bomb. If something is strong enough, maybe it can leave an imprint on wood and glass and stuff. Hard to see or hear, but there, you know?"

There wasn't another girl I knew of that I could imagine hearing this from. She began telling me about a girl who had died in their house before her family bought it. I listened two ways, hearing a ghost story and also following her voice's music. My arms sprouted chill bumps, and the movements of her mouth seemed to rhyme with something in my head and made me want to kiss her so badly it was painful. She looked at me and pushed her hair back, and on our third circuit I could see our trail in the weeds, yellow buds bowed towards the ground, stems at sharp angles, bleeding milk. Black grass seeds on our pants cuffs. I asked if it was a see-through ghost and felt her eyes on me, and she said she wasn't kidding, and I said neither was I, just curious, and she told me it was as solid as a person but suddenly just there or gone. And every few seconds our shoulders brushed accidentally, the way two people work a Ouija board without meaning to, and our fingers touched a few times, with the usual acrobatics of the heart, and in a little while we were holding hands somehow and talking very easily.

A car's headlights spun across us, and the car sped away. I saw with the driver's eyes this boy and girl holding hands in the park, and was able to believe it briefly. I put my free hand around her arm. She wrapped hers around mine. We locked together, trying to be one person instead of two, my pants feeling tighter and tighter.

"Are you afraid at night?" I asked. I was no longer sure of things. There could be ghosts.

Margie's hand tightened in mine. I squeezed back. She said, "Do you think I'm crazy?"

I touched, deliberately I guess, the razor scar on her wrist. My heart ached up into my throat. The wind fluttered around us now so that the park was all ripples and waves. Margie's hair floated. We stopped beside the tree and looked at each other a long time. Our faces were so close, and the sun so low, that I was able to see the faint gray inside her pupils.

"When you look at me that way," she said quietly, "I can hardly breathe."

I felt like I was risking my life. My head grew impossibly heavy and dipped a little. She slanted her face and lifted her chin and brushed her lips across mine, then opened her mouth. It happened fast, like accidents do. I remember a flash of panic such as in my dreams of smothering, and then, with a bird in an unseen fury above us, the sensation almost of eating, filling myself with warm gravy, and a loosening inside beyond what I knew could happen to me.

Then her face pulled away and I was as dazed as if I'd been punched. My stomach shivered. I held Margie and she laid her head against my chest. "Your heart is so loud," she whispered into my shirt. "Hey, next time bring me some of whatever you've been drinking."

The gum had failed. "Really? You drink?"

"Hell yes. Girls do a lot of regular things. Did you think I was tame?"

I relaxed all the way to my bones, farther. "Damn, I like you," I said, tightening around her thin, thrilling softness.

She nuzzled against my chest, giggled. "Damn, I like you too." Then she lifted onto her toes, and her eyes traveled down my face, and her mouth opened and the underside of her tongue pressed against her front teeth, and the mouth said finally, "Love you," and opened again over my mouth, and I felt it warm, soft, everywhere at once.

Southern Gothic

The next day must've happened, but I don't remember it. Waiting and boredom don't leave much to recall.

A slight drizzle began that evening, and it grew cooler, and I was able to justify the denim jacket I used to hide a quart of beer and carry it out of Riner's store. I drank it fast, with Margie, under the big magnolia in the park. We both still felt awkward, though. I suggested we sneak by my house and pick up some whiskey I had hidden.

When we got to my block, I let go of her in case any of the neighbors were spying. We walked down the lane, angering dogs, squares of light suddenly creating kitchen windows with wary silhouettes. Passing some yards, you smelled what the families had eaten for dinner. Inside my gate, a clothesline billowed with dampening laundry, my underwear dangling helpless.

"Carriage houses are so neat," Margie said.

Home suddenly looked fine, old brick, ivy.

I took hold of a pipe bolted to the rear wall and pulled myself up, hand over hand, ignoring the ache of my hernia, my sneakers grinding lichens off the brick. I crawled through my window and dug my whiskey jar out of the closet. I climbed halfway down, then dropped, Errol Flynn, absorbing the shock by bending my knees as I landed, Margie gasping at me.

We walked back down the lane. I unscrewed the jar, passed it to her, felt the voltage of her hand. She held the jar to her nose. "What is it?"

"Different whiskies, gin, vodka, Tia Maria. Whenever my dad opens a bottle, I skim some. For emergencies."

"Am I an emergency?" She held her hair back on one side, still smiling at me, and took several cat-sips, then pressed the back of her arm to her mouth, blinked slowly, surrendered the jar. "You're sweet," she said. "But that stuff tastes kind of gross."

I took a big gulp to impress her. Putting my lips on the threaded glass where hers had been gave me an excited, intimate feeling. I settled my arm around her shoulders, the hell with the neighbors, and she leaned into me and slid her arm around my waist and looked up like someone who trusted me completely. I felt the opposite of how I felt with boys. Her hair smelled wonderful, shampoo or perfume. Walking was difficult, but I didn't care.

"If you ever need a drink," she said, "you can come over to my house. We have a bar in the den with stools and all. Since my parents split up, they let me do whatever I want."

We swayed together to the park, the lighted mist like a shower of sparks in a foundry. Chills surged through me, and a pleasant drowsiness.

We crept inside the magnolia, a cave sweetened honey-and-lemon by the huge fleshy blossoms. The drizzle muffled everything. We sat against bark. Margie was dark shades of gray now, her face almost invisible, and my mind detailed the shadows so that she was even more gorgeous, unbearable. I told her she was beautiful.

"You are," she whispered back, face coming towards mine, and our mouths opened together, and I might as well have been

81

beautiful, I don't know, I couldn't have summoned my own name just then. I couldn't have said who Margie was, other than an eager mouth burning against mine, making tiny moans that stripped me of any thoughts at all, and I began to forget to be careful where I put my hands.

I eased away and sat back stunned and panting and un-ashamed against the tree trunk. Margie smoothed her sweater, flipped her hair back.

"I'll never be able to think about anything else." My voice seemed thunderous. I lifted the jar, sipped.

"You're all I ever think about. Kiss me again, please."

I was already moving towards her body heat.

After a while we just held hands. I felt so good that my mind sought something to worry over. This was habit. There must be something. Then it hit me, and I cleared my throat. "Margie?" Already sorry, I finished it. "Did Wade Madison kiss you at the Christmas bazaar?"

She sat up, and her hand went away. A drop of water smol-dered on the tip of a hand-sized leaf, distillation of the street-light.

"I was only ten. We didn't go together or anything. It was just once."

I started to tell her she was the only girl I'd ever kissed, stopped myself with another throat-clearing. Rusty had warned me about such honesty.

"Does that bother you a lot?" she asked, sounding farther away, emphasizing "that."

"Not too much," I said, though in my new greed I wanted explorer's rights, my flag only in this territory.

Margie's voice changed direction, "Oh," and I pictured her hugging her knees with her head laid on them. The water bead slid from the leaf, a tiny explosion of lights. "Because I've done a lot worse stuff than that," she said.

I waited. I made myself say, "What?"

I think she shook her head. "You'd hate me," she said. "No fooling. It's why I tried to kill myself." She found my hand and squeezed it hard.

"What?" I knew she wanted to tell me—that it was somehow necessary.

"Promise you won't hate me."

"Of course, I promise. You can tell me." I both did and didn't want to be told. I had nearly decided that she'd had sex with some boy.

"What?"

Margie was all shadow. The rain sizzled. A cricket chirped inside the tree with us. Then flatly she said, "I used to let my brother Donny do things to me, you know? Everything. I wanted to, at first. Now I hate myself."

A false soberness washed over me, leaving me without the ability to think. I felt like we were holding hands through the window of a train that was about to take her far away and forever. The nervous, stupid urge to laugh brushed past me. Then rage. I wanted to kill her brother, burn everything clean, die myself, end the world.

I was shaking. The drizzle washed the leaves.

I remembered to breathe, concentrated on that for a while.

And then the world expanded. Two kids with problems in a circle park weren't going to bring on the locusts or oceans of fire. They wouldn't even hold up traffic. Most of the anger breathed out of me, and my face, at least, grew used to it. I've never been able to stay angry. People think I'm understanding. I understand little. But I can bear almost anything, and that's nearly as good.

"I'm sorry, Margie," I said. "That's about the worst thing I ever heard."

"The first times we did it I felt like a saint, or a monster or something," she said. "I felt smarter than everybody else, and sort of dangerous. Then it started making me sick and I couldn't sleep and I felt like maybe I was possessed or something. I almost asked my mom to get a priest. Like in *The Exorcist.*" She made a hissing noise. "But I knew it was me. My fault. But I can't ever erase it. You probably hate me now, right? And I guess I'll go to Hell about twice over."

"I don't believe there is a Hell," I said. "And if there is, I'll be there too, and so will all my friends. Who cares?"

She exhaled. "You're nice, but I bet you already want to get away from me. I know what people must think, boys. Anyway, I deserve it."

Actually, she was partly right. I wanted to be away from her where I could think about this and decide how I felt and maybe get used to it. I strained towards logic. She'd been very brave to tell me, and I thought she must be feeling relieved, if not actually better. She needed me, then. Amazing. And it occurred to me, goose bumps making my scabbed legs hurt, that Margie was the only person who had touched me, for years, without using a belt or extension cord or fist. Feeling sorry for myself mixed in with feeling sorry for her, and something hooked in my chest.

"I'm glad you didn't kill yourself," I said. "And I'm glad you're not ordinary. I don't care about the other thing." That wasn't true, yet. But I hoped it would be.

"I was going crazy from keeping it secret. I had to tell you. I've been practicing what to say ever since that day in church when you smiled at me and I knew I still wanted to be alive."

She hung onto me and pressed against my shoulder, blinking back the tears. The ache in my throat spread into my face. Everything seemed so important. I pressed my lips to the damp hair over her ear and whispered that I loved her, and she clung to me harder, and then lights were shivering in my eyes.

I barely even sniffled, but Margie knew. She began to brush the hair back from my forehead and to kiss my cheeks. She stopped crying, whispered, "It's all right, baby, it's all right."

After a few seconds, of course, I realized how I must sound. I cut a sob in half, stopped. I sat back exhausted. "Damn it," I said.

"Man, am I embarrassed. What's wrong with me?" I was off guard and a reflex sniffle came out like a hog-noise. "Excuse me," I mumbled. "Don't ever hurt yourself again, okay, Margie? You're the only person I'm comfortable being humiliated in front of."

She giggled through a sniffle. "I started it. I'm more humiliated than you." She kissed my cheek. "Listen, I was too dumb even to kill myself right. I got the razor out of Mama's Gillette. The cuts on my wrists weren't much worse than the ones on my fingers from holding the razor. I fainted and hit my head on the toilet."

The idea of Margie's blood made me weak. We were wrapped around each other, sniffling in turn. It got abruptly dark. I assumed the streetlight had burned out. Dogs began to bark all over outside.

We talked about her parents' divorce. Also, she had an older brother in prison. I whined about my hernia and my parents beating me. We talked for I don't know how long. Finally she said, "Walk me home?"

We went out into the drizzle, every light in the neighborhood off. "It's mighty dark," I said. A flashlight beam floated over someone's backyard, shimmering with needles of rain. "The power must've gone out."

"Francis," Margie said, "what are you doing next weekend?"

"Well, I'm supposed to do something with the gang . . ."

"Oh. Because Mama's going out of town." Margie folded herself around me from behind, arms across my chest, chin on my shoulder, one thigh slid between mine. She spent a final sniffle. "I wish you'd find a way to come over and watch for the ghost with me. See if she's real or if I'm just crazy. Maybe it would make her go away. You could sleep in my room. I mean, if you want."

She held me in the dark. My face was cool from the rain. A few blocks away a siren bansheed and a whirling red light swept the treetops like fire. I raised my jar and sucked down the last burning trickle of liquor, and then I hurled the jar as hard as I could towards the street. After the burst there was a long tinkling sound as the jar disintegrated, the lid stammering across asphalt, and a long beam of light swung from a backyard towards the sound and made the pieces of glass glitter.

Precipitation and Anchovies

When I got to my yard I saw Tim hunched on the stone bench like a gnome, feet scissoring above the grass. I told him I had to go inside and get bitched out for being late. The streetlights had returned the familiar landscape, brought to mind the regular rules and punishments. My mouth was horribly dry, my clothes wet.

"I wouldn't grovel to my parents for a while," Tim said. "I smell booze on your breath from here." His hair strung over his eyes and ears, dripping water onto his Bogart-style trench coat.

I sat down beside him, further soaking my corduroys.

"You look ghastly, Francis. You didn't weep in front of that girl, did you?"

"Not so loud," I whispered. "My folks will hear us."

He hopped down and stood, trench-coated, and looked at the top of my head. He stretched himself, vertebrae spreading, neck thinning, until with the extra inch he was as tall standing as I was sitting. "Come on, then," he said. "We'll get something for your breath and hide out in my old clubhouse. You ever had anchovies?"

We shattered puddles on the way to Riner's store. Inside, some old men were drinking beer and shooting pool. A boy with bad acne bowed over the pinball machine in back, bumping it with his hip, slapping the flipper buttons, making bell-and-buzzer music. I slid the cooler open and pulled up a Coke while Tim ducked and shimmed a tin of anchovies into his sock. Mr. Riner, pistol holstered at his side, squinted at the fuzzy black-and-white TV at the end of the counter. He rang open the register, took my dollar. He was bald and had fingernails thick as nickels.

Tim always said that when you stole something, you actually paid for it with fear and worry, the currency of the outlaw.

Riner chuckled at something on *Hee Haw* and trickled coins into my upward palm.

We mushed through the lane into Tim's backyard. It was dense as a jungle. Tim's dad called it the only natural ecosystem in the neighborhood, but he kept the front lawn trimmed for his wife and for the neighbors. Frogs were singing.

The clubhouse, behind the garage, was five squares of plywood we'd dragged from the lumberyard one Sunday and hammered together. We opened the door panel, crouched inside. We sat on warped tea crates and Tim crackled the wrapper off the anchovy tin and started rolling it open with the key. The only light sprayed through a small galaxy of holes on one wall where Tim had tested his dad's shotgun. "So give me the filthy details," he said.

"There are none." My imagination was torturing me with a scene of Donny and Margie in bed, and when it got the most hideous (both of them naked and bucking, licking each other's mouths, sweaty, groaning), that little section stuck in an instant replay mode.

"Confess, man. I set you up in that cozy Maxfield Parrish scene. Share it for godsakes. I'll probably be a virgin until the day I shoot myself." Hints of fish came from Tim's corner. The buckshot holes speckled his face with light. He finished coiling the lid off the can. I recalled kissing Margie and my stomach ached.

"It's sort of private," I said, thinking even the good parts would spoil if exposed to another boy. "Who's Maxfield Parrish again?"

"Private? Shit, two days with a girl and friendship goes down the toilet. Fine. Then you'll never know why the electricity went out tonight."

"You didn't do that."

Tim smacked his lips. "Goddamn, these are tasty. Here, have an anchovy, get rid of that booze breath." He passed me the tin.

"What did you do to the lights?" I peeled a greasy strip out of the can and laid it in my mouth. I crunched prickly little bones. It tasted like a minnow half-dissolved in salt and oil. I gave them back to Tim and dug out my housekey and pried the cap off my Coke. I guzzled some, burped. "Those fish are corroded," I said. "Okay, I kissed her under the big magnolia tree again. We made out a little."

"And you started crying?"

"I didn't say that." I gulped more Coke, wiped greasy fingers on my knees. "It was part great, part awful. I can't say any more."

"Aw," he said. "My heart bleeds like a pig for you." He wadded a tiny fish into his mouth, snorted at me. " 'Can't say any more.' "

Rain drummed onto the flat wooden roof and dribbled down the inside walls, reviving the mildew smell. The frogs got louder.

"It's weird," Tim said quietly, chewing. "I'm not afraid of jack-shit. I'll take any dare, fight guys twice as big as me, I don't care. But the few times I've talked to a girl I liked—" He sucked a piece of fish from between his teeth. "—it's like my mind turned into a Hallmark card. And I get clumsy."

"Whatever's the most important is the most scary, I guess."

"Yeah, so," Tim said. "Are we going to trade secrets?"

"I can't."

"Please. It might be helpful to me."

"It's not. It's not a regular secret. Not normal."

"Oh, Jesus, now you really have to tell me. Come on."

"It wouldn't be right."

"Fuck! We've been best friends for three years. I taught you every interesting thing you know. I'm going to tell your mom you showed us her copy of *The Sensuous Woman* if you don't tell me."

"You would not, you bastard, you'd be ashamed."

"Please, I swear I won't tell."

"Not even Rusty?"

"Nobody. I swear. On William Blake's grave."

Telling it, I grew exhausted again and ashamed and then relieved, like going to confession myself. I meant to hold back the worst part, knew Margie didn't want it told, but it heaved itself up and then it was out in the clubhouse and sitting on Tim's back too. We were quiet. Tim took a deep breath and let it out whistling like a falling missile.

"You're right. You shouldn't have told me that," he said. "Are you bullshitting?"

"I wish."

The rain crashed for a while. Then Tim asked questions, shaking his head, studying me. He said, "It's one of those goddamn sick Southern things. You know, Edgar Allan Poe did it with his own teenage cousin. I forgive him, of course, he was a genius. Donny's just a putrid slug. Shit, you people." Tim crunched the final anchovy, swallowed, spit, held his hand out for the soda. I told him to finish it.

He turned it up and gurgled, passed the bottle back. "You can have the backwash."

I turned the bottle over and foam spattered into the dirt. I let the bottle thump to the ground. "What a world."

"Hell, you can comprehend it, though. Listen to those frogs. They're going to mate. You think they agonize about who's related to whom?" Tim creaked forward on the tea crate. "Let's say you're her brother—you've got this beautiful sister, you're comfortable around her, sleep in the same house—"

"Hush, man. Come on."

90

"Sorry. I'm willing to avenge this thing, just say the word."

"She avenged it on herself. Let's bury it, okay?"

"I envy you anyhow, you lucky bastard. Very romantic. Dark secrets, kissing under the lotus blossoms, ghosts . . . and what about this private pajama party you've got scheduled?"

"Tell me about the electricity now," I said. "What happened?"

"Oh. Nothing. I was bored. I took my axe and chopped down a utility pole. It didn't take two minutes."

"Jesus! Aren't we in enough trouble? Are you taking pills again?"

"Fuck!" Tim shot up and his head banged the ceiling and the clubhouse hopped and particles of something rained down my neck into my shirt. He swatted his leg, stomped, cradled his head, cursed.

"What?" I said, crouching up. "What!"

"A fucking big roach ran up inside my pants!" He peeled his jeans up over one knee, battered the door flat onto the grass, and tumbled out into the rain. I got out too. The clubhouse had shifted slightly, showing some bare earth and a stream of glistening cockroaches panicking into the grass towards the garage. "Gag a maggot," Tim said, standing, shaking out his trench coat. "You could rope and ride those sons of bitches." He unrolled his pantsleg. "Let's book on out of here and go see the wreckage."

We hauled Tim's bike out of the infested garage, and I pedaled with him sitting on the handlebars. On the black, shiny street the tires sprayed fans of water, flung grime up the back of my denim jacket.

Tim craned his head around so I could hear. "That power line snapped loud as a gunshot. Then total darkness, except for blue fire. The lemming types came out of their houses with flashlights. Going to light up the world with those flashlights, I guess." He laughed. "I stopped them all from watching *Happy Days*. Forced their IQs up a couple notches."

Two blocks away, people with umbrellas were ungrouping

from the entrance to the lane. A long truck occupied the entire curb, a jagged, weathered utility pole strapped inside its bed. We coasted up into a creosote smell.

A man in a hard hat was leaning out on a belt from the top of a new pole sunk beside the stump of the old one. He snipped and tied something and slid a tool into his pouch. Across the street, a CB radio growled and hissed inside a power company truck. A man with a hard hat and a devil sunburn stepped out and stared at us, began walking over. My mouth was as dry as if I'd sucked a green persimmon. I licked rain from my lips. I pedaled us out of the light and away, turning down a different street in case he was watching.

For the third or fourth time that week, I crackled with adrenaline. I doubled back, spun into Tim's front yard. He slid off the handlebars.

"Trouble is our only defense against boredom, Francis. You know that's the truth." He took the bike as I dismounted. "Look, tell your parents you're spending next weekend at my house. My parents are having that party Friday, so all the adults'll be occupied. You sneak away to Margie's, gain your manhood. Saturday, we camp in tents in my backyard and leave when it's dark to free the wildcat." He spit noisily. "The more dangerous life is, the better. Scary equals important, right?" He laughed and rustled away in his trench coat, walking the bike into the garage.

I pounded across the street and walked calmly in the front door, trailing footprints from my squishing sneakers. Daddy was sitting in front of the TV with a beer. A tiny Johnny Carson mimed a miniature golf-swing. I stood dripping, ready. Daddy turned his fist and frowned at his watch, sucked his teeth and ignored me. I slogged upstairs, stripped, and got into dry underwear.

In the bathroom I cupped my hands under the faucet and slurped water that seemed to have gushed over sugared ice. I couldn't get enough, my stomach swelled like a water balloon.

I brushed anchovy residue from my teeth and tongue. I had a couple of more swallows of water, then went and climbed into my bunk above Peter's snores. Gretchen's dog tags plinked.

The dry sheets felt wonderful and caused me to squirm, stretch. Rain pattered the window, and there was a casual boom of thunder which seemed to gather the whole world together, covering it like a giant blanket.

It rained most of the weekend, and I didn't see Margie.

Shopping on a Budget

The next night, while I was attempting to go to sleep, my brothers talked to each other from their bunks. They laughed at something, and Daddy came up the stairs with a beer in his hand and turned the light on. He said we were there to sleep, and that if he heard another peep out of us he was coming back with the belt and give it to us all. Then he went back downstairs to the late show and my mother. I didn't understand how he could've heard them unless he had the TV turned low and was listening out for us.

Looking back on these sort of incidents, I can only think that because their room adjoined ours it was important to them that we be asleep before they went to bed, if they wanted privacy. But all I knew at the time was that I drifted off to sleep that night with my brothers whispering, and abruptly the light was on and the sheet was stripped off me and my dad was slashing me awake with the belt. I judged him a cruel son of a bitch, Mama was guilty for allowing it, and if I was a juvenile delinquent I might as well blame it on that. The adult world was baffling and mean and I cared nothing for its laws.

We marched down Waters Avenue towards the shopping center. I had two large Rexall bags under my shirt, tucked into my pants, scratchy against my dampening belly. Rusty carried some old receipts and a ministapler to seal the bags after we'd filled them with supplies. Tim had loaned me sunglasses with tiny rearview mirrors inside each lens so that I could be the lookout. The mirrors were too small for details, but satisfied some James Bond notion we all held.

Joey, his thighs slushing each other as he tried to keep pace, panted, "Since this is my . . . first time . . . why can't I be lookout?"

Tim said, "You've got to swipe something to be in the gang. It's Francis's turn to be lookout. All you have to do is steal five small flashlights, okay? What else do we need?"

"Something to carry water in," I said.

Tim said, "Water's for sissies. We'll get some quart Cokes. The caffeine'll keep us alert."

Wade wanted candy bars. Rusty, beef jerky. Tim wanted to have sour pickles in the little bags with their own juice.

"Pickled pigs' feet," Joey added, blinking sweat behind his glasses.

"White people don't eat that stuff," Rusty said.

"As a gang member, if he wants pigs' feet," Tim said, "he's entitled."

Rusty snorted and dragged his shoes against the curb. The doctor said he had to wear them until they were worn out.

Tim said, "We're going to need green, brown, and black shoe polish to make ourselves invisible when we get to the island."

"For camouflage?" asked Wade. He tightened his triceps, peeking at his intermittent reflection in passing car windows.

"If the cops stop us," said Rusty, "I don't want incriminating shit all over my face."

"Nobody's even going to think of stopping me, because I'll be disguised as landscape."

The sidewalks ended and we walked on the grassy shoulder between the street and people's fences. Joey picked his nose, and each time he saw me notice he snuffled and rubbed his face like a bear and stuffed the hand in his pocket. Then his tics took over again, and the hand returned to its plunder.

We came to where a Spanish bayonet was growing out into the street. We maneuvered around it one at a time, cars swishing past on our left sides with a gritty breeze, thorn-tipped fronds aimed at us on the right. Each time one of us passed, we folded a frond over and pinned it through its own green flesh, as though the plant deserved to suffer for barring our way with its spikes.

I entered the Rexall first, alone, then the others drifted in, paired. I squeezed in behind the comic-book kiosk, and while Tim and Wade faked an argument at the record section, their curses drawing attention away from me, I slipped the shopping bags out of my shirt. Rusty strolled by and took them, grimacing at the designs left by my sweat.

I went to the next aisle and made a performance of reading shampoo labels, situated where I could watch half the store in the convex mirror mounted up in the corner. I saw fun-house versions of Tim and Wade wander over and accept a bag from Rusty. Then Rusty grabbed Joey's arm and steered him towards the hardware section. They passed a poster taped to the wall in imitation of a stop sign, a red octagon that said SROP! (Shoplifting Rips Off People!). I ducked back to reading labels, tried to decipher "hydrolized animal protein," wondered which one of these products made Margie's hair smell so nice.

I focused on the spy mirrors of my sunglasses. Behind me, a middle-aged woman pushed a shopping cart filled with party decorations. A boy my own age ran fingers through his feathered hair. A man, a vagrant, seemed to be staring at me. I got scared. I returned a bottle of shampoo to the shelf, then turned around. The man's eyes snapped over to a rack of packaged combs, and he pulled one off and meandered away.

Lifting a bottle of hair conditioner, I glanced up at the big fish-eye mirror. The man was staring at it from the next aisle, balloonish face, distant pin body. An all-over sweat squeezed out of me. I carried the conditioner past the man's aisle (he'd abandoned the comb) and walked by a twitching, grunting Joey and whispered that a man was following me. Joey blinked, shuttled over to Rusty.

I went all the way to the end of the store, into the hospital aroma of the pharmacy, and saw Tim slip a bottle of Calamine lotion into his swollen Rexall sack. He winked and left. I placed the hair conditioner on the nearest shelf. In my sunglasses rearview, I saw Rusty and Joey exit the store, Rusty laughing and flicking Joey's earlobe. Clerks, bothered by their horseplay, forgot to suspect them of stealing. I pursued Tim.

I heard a rhythmic slapping and turned around. The man was approaching me on noisy flip-flop sandals. I turned to the shelf, reaching for an alibi. Tampons, douche, feminine hygiene sprays. I chose a box of Summer's Eve, an outrageously flowery thing, and began building an explanation.

The man came at me, pulling from his back pocket a wallet thick as a deck of cards. It dropped open to a badge-and-ID centerfold which, through my shock, clued me he was a detective. He had a semibeard, weedy hair, and eyes so shot with red I thought of a junkie. His T-shirt was about ready for cleaning dipsticks.

"Okay, Bubba," he said, "how'd you like to take a little trip to the office with me?" His breath was a whiff out of a dumpster, and I stopped inhaling to prevent a gag.

I imagined myself in the juvenile home. I seemed to be momentarily upside down, some kind of terrified adrenaline hallucination. Caught, I remembered that I was technically innocent. I hadn't even *intended* to steal anything. I coughed to get my voice working. "I believe you made a mistake."

"Right. Where's that hair conditioner you had a minute ago?" He looked me over for telltale bulges.

I pointed at the bottle on the shelf. The man's hands slithered into his pockets and he began to bounce on his toes, glaring from side to side. I grabbed a breath.

"Look," he sneered, "I don't know what you got this time and what you didn't get." A mother and her knock-kneed toddler ambled up and the man crooked his head at a suntan-lotion display and led me over behind it. "I know what you're up to, okay?"

"Honest to God," I pleaded, and I actually felt misjudged. "I'm not stealing anything. My mother sent me to buy this—" I held up the douche (crucifix at a vampire) and saw the rush of color to his ears. "I thought I might have enough left over for the conditioner, but I don't." I nearly took off the sunglasses, for sincerity's sake, but didn't want to sacrifice their insulation. The man looked at the ceiling.

Wade swaggered past and the man's eyes tracked him. Wade walked out the door, and Tim hurried after him with the bag, yelling, "Wait, Jim, I want to buy some goddamn cigarettes!" Walking in, an elderly woman shook her head sadly.

"You know those boys?" The man wouldn't look at me. I began to feel sorry for him.

"I've seen them around," I said. "Maybe they were shoplifting while you grilled me."

98

He hissed. "I don't get paid enough for this bullshit. I ain't slept in three fucking days. Get out of here and don't let me see you again."

I figured leaving now was as bad as a full confession. He hadn't caught me in anything. I wanted to prove my honor, and also to relieve him of the feeling that I was getting away with something.

I flourished the box of douche again. "I have to buy this."

His ears blazed.

I walked to the checkout line, the detective's flip-flops slapping tile behind me. With my mirrors I watched him fold his arms over his chest so as to bulge his biceps, then lean against a post, watching me. I held the douche close to my leg near the counter as I waited in line. I tried to calculate the sales tax. The cashier was a pretty woman with sunflower earrings, and as I placed the box on the counter her eyes visited the detective, then settled on me. I blushed with several embarrassments. She smiled and worked the angry sounding cash register.

Twenty-one cents short. Each embarrassment was creating further embarrassment. I held out the money I had, said my mother hadn't given me enough.

"Well, let's see," said the woman. She lifted a nearby cup on which was written "Got a Penny, Give a Penny—Need a Penny, Take a Penny" and emptied it into her hand. She counted nineteen cents. Beside me, a man's arm turned a wristwatch upright. Another man cleared his throat. Others, inspired, cleared theirs. Summer's Eve waited on the counter. Sweat trickled down my ribs like a crawling insect. "Hold on," the woman said and lifted a purse from beneath the counter.

The man behind me said, "Here you go," and clicked a nickel impatiently onto the counter. The register chimed open, the girl spilled in the money, gave me two cents change, and said, as she stapled the douche into a bag, that she liked my sunglasses. I offered the pennies to the man. "Keep them for next time," he said. I clinked them into the cup and forced a smile at the woman.

Slain with humiliation, I trudged out, the doors swinging open violently as I stepped on the plastic mat. None of the gang had lingered outside, so I headed roundabout towards Rusty's, where I knew they'd be. Outside a bakery I passed an empty police car, windows down. I ripped the brown paper off of the box and chucked the douche onto the driver's seat. A voice quacked loudly on the radio, sending needles into my heart. I walked half a block on dissolved knees, then jogged through the lanes.

As usual, the air conditioning in Rusty Scalisi's house was so extreme you could see your breath. His dad was out surf casting at the beach, and his mother was shopping. Tim, Rusty, and Joey were spreading the loot out on Rusty's bed. His room was very neat, with sports equipment stacked all along the walls. Over his bed was a big painting of dogs playing poker.

I explained what had happened with the detective, and Joey said he was glad he hadn't been the lookout after all. "Damn," he said, "this must be a hundred dollars worth of stuff."

Rusty said, "I had to threaten him to get him to steal the flashlights, but after he saw how simple it was, he wanted everything in sight. Look at these comics. *Richie Rich, Archie, Romance.* Who's gonna read that crap?"

I estimated sixty comics in the garish fan across Rusty's pillows. Joey had simply pulled three or four random stacks off of the rack, duplicates and all.

"Yeah, you've got to be selective, Joey," said Tim. "All that risk deserves better than *Richie Rich.*"

"There's a *House of Mystery,*" I said. "I'll take that if nobody else wants it."

We helped Rusty hide the loot in his footlocker, then sat around talking and reading and getting chilly. *Richie Rich* wasn't so bad, actually. Tim got Rusty to call the orphan drug pusher he knew, about getting some angel dust, which is actually animal tranquilizer. Rusty said we could get it on Friday.

The doorbell rang and Rusty let Wade in. He was breathing hard, his nostrils pinching and dilating. He had his green canvas bookbag.

"What've you got?" I asked. The grins from the others meant they knew.

Wade said, "I stole it during a funeral Mass. I walked into the sacristy like I belonged there and took it." He turned his bag over on the bed and a bottle of sacramental wine rolled out, followed by a baggie bulging with Eucharist wafers.

Joey said, "Man, y'all are going to burn in Hell."

"So are you," said Wade. "But we'll travel with trail mix from Heaven."

Rebels of the
Blessed Heart

Father Kavanagh had cancelled his weekly hour of Religion with our class. I suspected it was because seeing "the artists" would bring to mind images from *Sodom vs. Gomorrah '74,* in much the same way as I was afflicted by watching Margie's brother Donny, sunken into the desk in front of mine, pulling at a scab on his neck.

We'd been ordered to read silently. *The Return of Tarzan* was open on my desktop, but the pictures in my head were of Margie, Margie and me, Margie and Donny. I squirted a third layer of glue onto my left palm, spread it with my right finger, sucked the finger clean. It tasted vaguely plastic. I'd heard it was made from animal hooves. I blew on the hand and Elmer the Cow glared from the Glue-All label.

Sister Rosaria, twirling a Kleenex-sheathed finger in her nostril, said, "All right, class. Take out your history texts." She inspected the tissue, then dropped it with the others in the wastebasket.

The classroom rustled and scraped, books slapped. Tim laid *1984* inside his history book and continued to frown into it.

The nun piped, "Who can tell me why there's a historical marker at St. John's Episcopal Church?"

Two hands floated. Eric Johnson, the doctor's boy, and Donny Flynn, his arm in a plaster cast decorated with swastikas and peace symbols. The answer to the question was undoubtedly a war. It was Donny's only topic of interest.

Eric knew everything. Rosaria called on Donny.

Donny dropped his arm pow! on the desk and said, "It was General Sherman's headquarters."

Rosaria bared coffee-stained teeth. "That's right. Yes. Good."

To compensate, Donny slouched back again in the juvenile delinquent mode, arms hanging.

Rosaria slipped on her harlequin glasses and then wrote WILLIAM TECUMSEH SHERMAN on the green chalkboard behind her. "During the Civil War, Sherman marched his troops here from Atlanta, setting fire to everything along the way until he came to the sea. He spared Savannah because of its beauty and gave it to President Lincoln for Christmas. That's why we have so many Victorian houses left." She clapped beige dust from her hands, sat.

We'd studied the Civil War already this year. I believe Rosaria was trying to nurse race relations, because of the purse-snatcher killing, and the duck.

Rosaria asked who'd read *Gone With the Wind*, or seen it, and a sudden crop of right hands sprang up. I'd sneaked into the movie a couple of years before with Tim and Rusty. I enjoyed Vivien Leigh's bosomy gowns, but the story wearied me like the soap operas. It was a tourist-shop picture of the South, unreal to me.

I ignored the nun's whiny praises of Margaret Mitchell. I stared around and imagined various girls out of their clothes. Angie Sipes chewed on her pen, licking at the cap between little bites. My stomach ached to think of the activities you might get a girl to agree to. I was scheduled to spend Friday night with Margie, but I found I couldn't imagine anything carnal between us, as if she was too pure to be thought about that way. Odd, especially since I couldn't help but picture her with Donny.

Rosaria droned. Beside me, Tim and Rusty exchanged pellets of paper. Behind us, Wade had his head close to the desktop, sketching a wildcat with muscles so well-cut it looked skinned.

The windows were cranked open and from time to time bees wavered inside, hovered, then streaked down and across the street to where the azalea bushes were exploding lavender, pink, and white, and the bees became specks darting in and out of the blossoms.

"Let's open our texts to page 161," Rosaria said, and a general scrape and the faint crack of book spines resulted.

A generic watercolor adorned that page, soldiers in blue conquering soldiers in gray. But the figures on my copy dangled giant penises drawn in black ink, and several had painted lips and long lashes. They exhaled balloons filled with vile dialogue. I flipped the page so Rosaria wouldn't see. Across the next two pages, in bold Magic Marker, were the words ROSARIA SUX HIPPO DIX. I rested my arms across the words. Rusty and Tim snickered.

Slowly, I tore the pages out with my unglued hand, hoping to finish before Rosaria strolled the aisles. I wadded the pages into my pocket.

The nun said, "Francis Doyle," and my pulse stopped. I grimaced up at her and she said, "Please read aloud beginning on 161."

"I can't, Sister," I said. "My pages are missing."

She made me bring my book up. She soured her face over it, ran her finger along the serrations. "It looks as if someone deliberately tore this," she said. I was reflected mite-like in her glasses.

"I bought it secondhand."

"All right. Look on with someone else."

I scraped my desk over beside Tim's.

Rosaria said, "Not with Tim Sullivan."

I scraped back against Rusty's desk. Rosaria stared disgustedly, but allowed it.

104

The same pages were torn from Rusty's book, and the next two were psychedelic from squiggly lines he'd used to camouflage what Tim and Wade had drawn there.

"Chuck Spinnett," Rosaria said, "you have a nice reading voice. You begin."

Chuck commenced. He had a mild speech defect, due partly to the wires and rubber bands on his teeth. He slurred through *Manassas, Antietam,* and *Shiloh.* After, Rosaria said, "Class, this was the bloodiest war ever fought in the Western Hemisphere, ten times as bad as Vietnam. Now why was our country divided against itself in 1861?"

The air boiled with hands. None of them belonged to our gang. It was such a recycled subject that even Joey O'Connor abstained. I noted that the mood rings on the Kelly twins' fingers had turned different colors.

Rosaria called on Craig Dockery, Negro, breaker of duck wings.

"The Civil War was on account of the people didn't want to free the slaves like Lincoln say they had to."

"*Said,*" corrected Lewis Epps, the darkest boy in the school.

"Very good, Craig," said the nun.

Donny Flynn stood up, unasked. "The South wanted to succeed from the unions but the Feds wanted to control everything." Craig cut his eyes at Donny.

"Yes, there was a matter of secession. But slavery is a stain on our past. The Confederacy was a lost cause even before it began."

Donny Flynn sneered. Craig Dockery elevated his chin at Donny.

Rosaria continued. "God inspired men like Abe Lincoln and U. S. Grant to look into their hearts and do what was best for mankind."

Tim said, "If God was on the Union side, why'd it take them four years to slaughter an army they outnumbered four to one?"

Rosaria blinked. "God doesn't interfere with free will."

"Oh. Maybe you should mention the part where Lincoln offers

Robert E. Lee command of the Union Army, but Lee turns it down to defend the South, even though he doesn't own slaves, or that Grant was an alcoholic and a corrupt president—" Tim had folded his arms across his chest and was speaking rapidly in his Northern preemptive fashion, with Dockery and Flynn both muttering, then Tim raising his volume, "—and Sherman was insane, which made him good at setting fires and exterminating American Indians—"

"Well, I didn't want to bring all that in at an eighth-grade level," barked Rosaria, hoisting herself up and scowling like a beacon. "In fact, Lee and Grant were both gentlemen—"

"But weren't the slaves freed in the North mainly so they could fight?" All the heads swung to Tim, straining forward in his desk. "And Lincoln was willing to let Southerners keep their slaves if they'd give in to the Union—"

"That may be partly true!" All heads swung back to the screeching nun. She raised herself onto her toes and tilted forward, leaning on the desk. "But let's not stray into conjecture! Everyone's father isn't a history professor, Mr. Sullivan! The slaves were freed and—"

"Stayed on as dirt-poor sharecroppers—"

"They were free!" Rosaria shrilled, face purpling. I'd seen some spit fly at us. The students all whispered, mumbled.

Tim relaxed into his seat. "Right. They could starve or get lynched. And meanwhile the South gets turned into a backwards hog wallow."

Rosaria swung out from behind her desk and was lumbering down the aisle towards Tim. "If I were a little boy as small as you, I'd listen—"

"I do some outside reading so I'll know what's what."

Rosaria slapped the wood of Tim's desk. Craig cocked his chin as high as it would go, iced his eyes, and said, "Is he tryin to say slavery was supposed to be all right?"

Lewis Epps rolled his eyes. Tim flung his head as if dizzy and

106

said, "Craig, don't leave your brain to Science." Donny turned to Craig and said, "I'd chain you up in a heartbeat," laughed. The whole class was chattering. Craig snarled, "Kiss my mother—"

"Class!" Rosaria screamed, smacking Tim's desk again, lines radiating from her eyes, her mouth. We got quiet.

She continued the lecture in a more detailed, qualifying way, but Tim was uninterested now. He was toiling over two scraps of paper with two different pens. He printed one in black, the other in sloppy green cursive. Both were a jumble of misspellings, abuses of grammar, and unnecessary quotation marks. A series of racial and sexual insults, in toilet-bowl language, challenged a fight on the softball diamond at lunch.

"Get this one onto Donny's desk," Tim whispered and gave it to Rusty. "I'll plant the other one with Craig."

I felt guilty about it, of course. Donny was Margie's brother, his arm was broken. And Craig was black. I stressed this in a half-sincere appeal to Tim, knowing he didn't want to seem prejudiced.

"Prejudiced against what? Sadistic assholes? Think about that duck screaming, think about Flynn delivering our comic book to Kavanagh. And Margie." He raised his eyebrows. "I'll bear full responsibility."

When we were dragging out our English books, Tim pelted Craig in the neck with the folded note. Rusty had just delivered Donny's.

They read them. Craig ripped his savagely and slung it across to the wastebasket and began massaging his arms. Donny waited for a quiet moment, then blew his nose into the note. Throughout the period they reminded me of tomcats yowling from opposite sidewalks, separated by a busy street, their backs humped and electrified.

I peeled the dried glue off finger by finger, and a cool relief filled my hand. I laid the translucent handskin on my desk. It was whorled and banded with the map of my identity, fingers spread. Stop, it seemed to be saying, or Help. With felt-tip pens, I colored it extravagantly, fingers like a peacock's tail, a strange face on each tip. I divided the palm into green earth and blue sky, drew clouds wearing smiles and sunglasses, trees bearing rainbow fruit, skulls, crosses, dinosaurs, stars, and ringed planets.

It blazed from my desk, and people looked. A universe shed from my hand, the brightest spot in the room.

✝

All the boys ate furious lunches.

I jogged to the park. The grass was lacquered with the weekend's rain, and the orange clay of the softball diamond had changed into soup. Donny and Craig were rolling, surrounded by shouting boys. Craig pinned Donny in the mud and sat on his chest. Both looked as if they'd been slopped with orange paint. Donny slugged Craig in the kidneys, his cast adding weight to the blows. Craig smacked him in the forehead. Black skin gaped out of Craig's torn shirt-sleeve.

Donny's face contorted like he was crying, but without tears. Craig, breathing hard, studied him coldly. "Awright," Craig said. "You give? I'll let you up, you promise to walk away. We're finished?" Craig poised his fist over Donny's nose.

"Okay!" Donny groaned, wincing. "Okay."

Craig got off of him. Donny sat up and wiped mud out of his eyes. Craig tried to scrape the slop from his knees, gave up, tucked his shirt in, and swaggered away towards the water fountain.

Donny snarled and charged at him, Craig spun around and began to slip, and Donny whacked him across the eyes with his plastered arm, and the cast cracked in two. Craig grabbed

Donny's collar and the shirt ripped open as they both splattered down.

Their faces were horrible, rage and pain, the clumsy ugliness that makes you want to stop a fight. All the boys went "Ooooh . . ."

Craig and Donny locked together on the ground, panting, and traded spasms of short, halfhearted punches. Then they lay there. Donny slowly worked his elbow around Craig's jaw, achieving a headlock. Craig pretzeled Donny's invalid arm up behind his back with the broken cast hanging on it. Their legs squeezed, relaxed, squeezed. Donny looked as if someone had mashed berries against his lips, and Craig's left eyebrow had a raw spot. They exchanged little punches, paused, hit.

Tim, on the other side of the ring, stepped forward and stooped beside them. "I just wanted you two pinheads to know that I'm the one who sent you those notes." He laughed, spit. Craig and Donny held each other.

Then Craig writhed free and scrambled, sliding, and Tim bolted and Craig ran after him. They ran figure eights around the field, Tim in quick bursts so that the larger boy reached out and snatched air as Tim ducked and doubled back, dodged behind the cyclone fence, laughed.

Craig stopped and bent over with his mouth wide, resting his hands on his knees. He looked at each of our gang, his yellowed eyes slit, first at Rusty, who waited with his head cocked and hands on his hips, then at Wade, as tall as Craig and flexing the cords in his forearms. Craig looked at me, straightened up, walked over. He knew I was the least dangerous.

My blood burned. My legs shook. I didn't know, at that age, that adrenaline always makes you shake if you don't spend it immediately. I had never fought a black kid, and never anyone that powerful. The shaking made me feel twice as cowardly.

Donny was hammering his cast against the metal fencepost,

clang! clang! crunching the orange-smeared plaster into startling white pieces, then crumbling them from his arm.

"Why y'all think you're so bad?" Craig asked me.

"I don't," I said. "I have a hernia." I turned my back on him
and started walking away.

He grabbed my shirt at the shoulder and said, "I axed you a
question!"

I whipped around and my shirt pulled out of his fist, the
cotton smudged rusty, and Craig began to shuffle, throwing
his fists out loosely and swinging them in a circle, chanting
"Rope-a-dope, rope-a-dope." It was a silly, affected display which
nonetheless gave me time to consider the thinness of my arms
and the new difficulty of filling my lungs. All faces were turned
towards us. Rusty and Wade stood with fists balled, but etiquette
required them to stay put until I was injured. Voices urged us
to fight.

The secret baby inside me began bawling that this was un-
fair, ordering me to run, to beg Craig not to hurt me. I kept my
mouth shut, though, and my face reasonably tough.

I gave him my back again. He shoved me, and my neck whip-
lashed.

I wheeled and banged him in the mouth, felt his teeth nick
my knuckles. He touched his lips, surprised. I was shocked and
exhilarated. Then I wished I had hit harder, and again, because
he'd already recovered. My classmates made noises of doom.

Curtis Simms, another black eighth-grader, stepped towards
us. Rusty drifted nearer, and Wade. Blue-black Lewis Epps. Hurley, the white athlete. The black seventh-graders were coming.

Then I was stumbling, clouds and sky vivid and whirling,
Craig's eyes crazy and his fist recoiling. The skin around my eye
was swelling, kept swelling, and I feared it would burst. I pressed
my hand to my cheek and felt liquid, looked at my fingers. Clear
fluid, not blood. I had become biology, not me, just a body in
animal peril.

Craig grew bigger fast. "Come on! I'll black your other eye!"

I felt weaker, but dulled. Disgusted that this huge kid wanted to harm me. You can't hurt me, I thought, this isn't really me.

Wade and Rusty both jumped Craig, and they all fell into the mud together.

Black Curtis Simms launched at Tim, and they fell grappling, biting, and clawing. I couldn't stand the looks on their faces.

Everywhere, boys paired up and fell slithering through the mud, like salamanders. Wade's little brother, Steven, was grinding some boy's face into it. White boys were shoving white boys. I thought I saw two blacks fighting, the clay made it hard to tell. Beside me, Joey O'Connor was tussling with an anonymous orange kid who probably weighed half as much as him. Joey was a tongue-chewer. Three pink inches jutted out between his teeth. A hard uppercut from the other kid would cause him to bite off his tongue. Joey's eyeglasses were spattered blind. Through my confusion, I was afraid for him.

Then I saw that every blow being landed around me was to the body. The brawl had grown epic, spectacular, but beyond danger into wrestling. The faces had turned from ugly to comic. It was a herd of boys roughhousing in the mud.

Lewis Epps, minus his shirt, stumbled into me hard and I shoved him off and he sat in the slop. He got up, and I made automatic fists, and he charged and hugged my ribs and hoisted me off my feet and we toppled, splashing into it. Clay squished under my waistband, my collar. We rolled, churned, then stopped and looked at each other from an inch away. There was mud on the hairs in his nose. I couldn't recognize him.

"What the hell?" I said, tasting clay.

"I don't know." His breath was on my face. "I'm supposed to serve a funeral Mass after recess."

We untangled and started dragging people apart. Some allowed it, others made me feel like a hockey referee. They'd ignore you, roll over your feet, push you away. I found that if I

111

shouted, though it hurt my hernia, they ceased. "The teachers are coming!" I yelled, cleaving apart boys I couldn't identify.

"Here come the teachers," bellowed Lewis Epps.

Boys rose, smirked, and searched for sucked-off shoes. They wiped their faces and flung clay from their fingers. My cheek was throbbing, my hand ached. Tim passed, slapping me on the splattery back.

"Young Henry Kissinger," he said. "Diplomat. Francis, man, you slay me."

Tim limped over to Craig, who was propped against the fence, straightening the tatters of his shirt.

"Look at my clothes," Craig said. "You're in for it, man."

"I don't give a damn what you think about me, Craig. You're a bully. You like to hurt anything that can't hurt you back. That's why you hit that duck, and that's why you went after Francis instead of the other guys. And that's the same attitude the slave traders had when they held a gun on your ancestors and forced them into a cage. Think about that for a while."

"You might know books, little man, but you don't know what's in my mind." Craig licked his lip where blood was hardening.

Tim cleared his throat and spit on the ground. "You've got a big blob of clay on your head, Dockery."

"You got some on your chin."

They wiped clay off. Tim shrugged and walked over to me and we plodded towards our oak tree.

A mud-covered tribe of boys was playing lazy soccer, easy soft-ball. Rusty smiled down at his orthopedic shoes, which appeared to be finally ruined. Margie was sitting over on the bleachers. I waved. She waved.

Tim lay on the ground with his ankles crossed, fingers laced behind his head. "Don't worry, Francis," he said. "She knows Donny gets beat up all the time. You ever, ever seen him without stitches or a cast or crutches?"

"His one arm is all shriveled and small," I said. "Reminds me of a fiddler crab."

"Anyhow," said Rusty, "he got us into boocoos of trouble. I'm sorry I didn't get to fuck him up personally. Hell, he molested his own sister—" Rusty halted, looked past me, coughed, pulled at a seedling and studied it.

"Molested?" said Joey.

I was drained with anger. "You promised!"

"Well, Rusty *is* godfather of the gang." Tim met my eye. "I'm sorry, man, it preyed on my mind. I had to tell, just like you had to tell, and Margie too. That's why confession was invented." He sighed.

I hurried across the field, the street, into the school building, the lavatory. I got out of my shirt and soaked it in the sink. I anointed myself with water, dried with paper towels, wrung out the shirt. All the wrinkles were orange, in the shirt, my face, my elbows.

The teachers quizzed us about the clay, black eyes, bloody lips, and we blamed it on soccer and softball. They couldn't do anything.

For the rest of the day I didn't speak to anyone. After the bell, I ran home.

Pets

A day could be salvaged by something in the mail. A fat khaki envelope loomed out of the mailbox, and at first I thought Kavanagh had sent the awful comic book to my parents. But it was addressed to me, from TranScience Co. I ran upstairs with it, tore it open, spilling some kind of padding like minced newspaper.

Inside, a cardboard panel showed a family of pink, smiling Sea Monkeys, and below were three plastic windows containing numbered packets. I shook the envelope upside-down and a leaflet flapped out, "It's Fun to Raise Pet Sea Monkeys."

In the painting the Sea Monkeys frolicked amid bubbles and seaweed. Their backs were finny, they had fleshy crowns on their heads. In the background others waved from the parapets of a submerged castle. A boy Sea Monkey rode bareback on a green manta ray. Beside the packets, in eye-strain print, it said "Caricatures are not intended to depict artemia salinas."

TranScience Co. was betting that most kids didn't even know what "caricature" meant, let alone the Latin words. *Artemia salinas* was the animal, whatever. I didn't really expect any kind of monkey for $1.35.

The handbook revealed they were brine shrimp.

Shrimp filled Savannah's creeks every summer. Some grown man in a tie had probably spent weeks devising an ad campaign to trick kids into buying shrimp to raise in a jar. Adults can legally screw children out of their money, and are considered successful businessmen.

I found a pickle jar we'd been using for a glass and measured some water into it. Our dachshund, Gretchen, followed me around the kitchen, laying her paw against my leg whenever I was still. She wanted treats.

The handbook informed me that to create "Instant Life" I must let their "Water Purifier" act on the water for twenty-four hours. I opened the packet and poured what I suspected was standard sea-salt into the water, clinked a spoon around in it.

I investigated the pantry and located a bag of Chips Ahoy cookies on the top shelf behind the box of electrical fuses and batteries. I slipped a cookie to the dog, then carried the bag upstairs with the jar of water. I sat the jar on my chest of drawers. My middle brother, John, came up and peeked in the doorway. "Sea Monkeys," I said, and his eyes got wide, and I walked out as he walked in and went to the jar to try and see them.

Without allowing myself to think, I confronted the telephone, put the receiver to my ear. I touched the phone book and remembered the Flynns' number. I'd only managed to call Margie once before, to arrange a meeting in the park, because I was afraid Donny would answer and guess, or know, that I knew what he'd done with his sister. Each digit I twirled compounded my anxiety, and each time it rang was an electric jolt.

"Hello," said Donny's voice.

I hung up.

I forced myself to dial again.

Someone answered, breathed a while. "Yeah, hello?"

"May I please speak to Margie?"

"Who's this?"

After a sick surge, like dropping fast in an elevator, I realized

115

I wasn't doing anything wrong. "Francis Doyle."

"Did you just call and hang up?"

"I thought I'd dialed wrong."

"Oh. Hey, that fight was unreal today, wadn't it? Tell Sullivan his ass is grass. Hold on." He shouted, "Margie!" so loudly it hurt my ear. The phone clicked, slight static crackled on, an extension being picked up. A hand squeaked over a mouthpiece. A muffled girl's voice said, "I got it," then the hand squeaked off.

"Hey," I said.

Margie said, "Donny, get off the goddern line!" Click. "Um, sorry. What's wrong? I saw you running home today."

My insides plunged again. I asked how she was. She asked about my black eye. I amplified the pain so she'd feel sorry for me. She said she'd make it all better and asked me again what was wrong.

"I have to tell you," I said, "but I don't want to. I'm afraid you'll hang up and never speak to me again." I thought if I predicted her worst possible reaction, some voodoo would prevent it. "I sort of told Tim the secret you told me. He told Rusty."

With a little hurt gasp, she hung up. After a few centuries of dial tone, I hung up too.

Lacking any experience with girls, I assumed she was done with me forever. I dragged myself back into my room and crawled up into my bunk and clamped the pillow over my head, feeling like a dead fish with its insides scraped out, eyes clouding. The phone rang. I flung myself out of bed, catching my foot in the quilt, wrenched somewhat slowly to the floorboards and hurt my elbow, then threw the quilt off and stumbled out to the phone. I captured it on the fifth ring. "Hello?"

"I hate you," Margie said, voice pouty, injured, but not hateful, and my heart stirred some.

"I'm sorry," I said. "Don't hang up. I'm sorry. I can't think what to say. I love you."

Then a while of breathing, a radio on somewhere in her

house, a sigh, *Gilligan's Island* repeating downstairs, ice cubes tinkling in a glass on Margie's end. Maybe it was only a second.

"You shouldn't tell boys about private things between you and a girl. And you shouldn't tell girls awful things on the phone, Francis Doyle. You're supposed to do it in person, in case you have to make up, after."

I considered this a stay of execution. I said I was sorry at every opportunity.

"Stop saying you're sorry. And you can tell your friend Tim I'm mad at him too. Donny has to get a new cast put on his arm." She was quiet for a second. "He's still my brother."

"Would it be okay if I met you at the park tonight?" I didn't feel right saying this, and I was relieved when she said no.

"If you want to make it up to me, you can stay over Friday night and keep watch for the ghost."

"Then you'll have to say you forgive me now. That way I can forgive Tim, and then I can tell my parents I'm spending the night with him. Okay, please?"

"I might think about it."

"You know, if you really hated me, I'd die. You're the only thing in the world."

"Don't try to make me cry."

Because she was angry and pouty and my attachment to her was in jeopardy, I wanted her badly, physically, and my pants grew snugger, warmer. I stared at my poster of Neil Armstrong planting a flag on the moon. We wrangled about who had to hang up first. I submitted.

I ate the entire bag of chocolate chip cookies. At dinnertime I pretended to be sick. Mama came up and took my temperature and gave me aspirin for my eye and knuckles. Her concern seemed larger than my condition. I lay in bed and finished the Tarzan book.

✝

After the birds started, I got up and opened the packet of Sea Monkey eggs, little aqua-tinted crystals which had probably sat in some warehouse for years. The water hadn't cured for twenty-four hours, but I decided to risk it.

Still in my underwear, I flipped my curtain back so a beam of sunlight sliced through the jar of water. I poured in the crystals, tapping the packet to get them all out safely. For one minute, as instructed, I stirred the water with a pencil. My brothers slept. The dog whined in a dream.

Downstairs, in the coffee-smell, the television murmured the early news update. Tomorrow's black protest march. Watergate. Skylab. A Mexican scientist claimed a cure for cancer. Partly cloudy. Daddy coughed.

I stopped stirring, put my face close to the jar. Dozens of tiny whitish dots were flicking around in the water. Live creatures, hatched on my dresser, that minute. You can be amazed by nothing more than brine shrimp. I felt suddenly like that first sailor who stepped off a ship's ramp onto the dried lava of the Galapagos, awed by the acres of tortoises and iguanas. I peeled the corner off the third packet and tapped out a few grains of food. They would eat. They would grow. They'd require care and responsibility. Someday I'd have to take them to the ocean, set them loose. In the jar the tiny shrimps clustered towards the spike of sunlight.

The next few days were what we called Machine Gun Days. Those are days when you wish you could take a machine gun and wipe out everybody you see. Tim and the gang left me alone. Thursday night Margie called me, and while my little brothers listened on the kitchen extension, she blessed me with her official forgiveness, and I forgave the rest of the world and surrendered my machine gun attitude.

Food Chain

Friday morning, as planned with the gang, I skipped school. I shrugged my uniform on, swallowed milk, walked Peter school-ward, and then navigated the lanes back into our house. The dog was the only witness to my return. I cocooned myself in bed and went back to sleep. A racket at the window scared me awake, and I rolled over and shoved my face through the curtain.

Gravel spattered the metal screen. I jerked back. Tim was standing in the lane, hooking his arm for me to come down.

I stumbled below to the kitchen and opened the back door. Tim stepped in, then backed out, and held a one-second finger up. He hawked and spit, followed me upstairs.

My mouth tasted garlicky, and I felt empty and irritable.

"We're the only ones skipping," Tim said. "Rusty has to serve the school Mass this afternoon. Get dressed for adventure." Tim's hair was shagged out over his ears, and he wore cuffed jeans and a sweat shirt he'd silk-screened with a Picasso bull. He tapped my jar of Sea Monkeys. "These are just brine shrimp, you know."

"What makes you think I want to speak to you?"

"You came downstairs in your underwear and let me in. Be-sides, you're not capable of staying mad more than a couple days.

By the way, I saw Kavanagh walking into the principal's office with the dread manila envelope yesterday. I hope we haven't waited too long." He opened my closet and rummaged. "Where's your whiskey jar?"

"Margie and I drained it." I dragged yesterday's corduroys off the dresser and yanked them on. "You're not drinking this early?"

"If I give myself a liquid lobotomy by 10 A.M. I might Have A Nice Day like all the other idiots. It keeps me from throwing firebombs."

I pulled a T-shirt on, mumbling through fabric, "You won't live long."

"Adulthood doesn't interest me. My only worry is drinking'll stunt my growth."

I went into the bathroom, flipped the light on, and a transistor radio hummed awake on the back of the toilet. This entertained my mother during the hours she spent concocting her face and hair. The music, all strings and choruses, tried eerily to be soothing.

The mirror reminded me that my blackened eye had faded into bluish yellow. My hair stood up like a flame because I'd used my pillow that morning as a substitute for nighttime. I stroked it down with a brush, but it rose halfway again. I doused it with water.

Tim peeked in. "When you finish fagging-off with your hair, we're thumbing out to Ferguson House to buy the angel dust."

Ferguson House was the boys' home out in the country. Tim said we were going to meet with the orphan kid who stayed with Rusty's family one weekend a month. The boy would sell us PCP, an animal tranquilizer.

"They use it in Jellystone—I mean Yellowstone," Tim said, "to knock out grizzlies."

"Why are we thumbing all that way? Let's ride bikes."

"It's easier to avoid the cops on foot. You can't hop fences with thirty pounds of bicycle."

In the lane we picked wild blackberries, tiny thorns dragging at our fingers like kittens' claws. We ate them, and the seeds revenged themselves between our teeth. Tim spat purple. We crossed the street to Riner's store. I stepped on the exact spot where my brother John had bled onto the sidewalk after the car hit him. For weeks afterward, kids had made pilgrimages to see the stain. Now it was just indifferent concrete.

Tim said, "Let's rev up our nervous systems with a Coke. My treat."

I waited outside so Mr. Riner wouldn't mention truancy next time Daddy was in for a six-pack. On the door was a hand-lettered sign Riner had posted when blacks moved into the neighborhood: ONLY 2 STUDENTS ALLOWED IN STORE AT 1 TIME. Riner trusted our whole gang, however, and we stole from him with friendly regularity.

Tim stepped out, shoving the door open with his foot. He handed me a sweaty, uncapped bottle. I turned it up, swallowed many times, and belched vigorously.

"If only we could harness that as a source of energy," Tim said. He took small sips because he didn't know how to burp.

We walked along Waters Avenue, wary of police cars. We finished our Cokes, leaving a finger of backwash, and hid the thick emerald bottles in a bed of ivy, for when we needed change.

We talked movies, books, school. I stuck on the topic of Margie Flynn so long that Tim asked me to shut up. The day was warm and green, with birds singing at the edges. Each time a car approached, Tim aimed his thumb down the road.

A Lincoln Continental, going the opposite way, slowed past

us. It U-turned and overtook us, slid up on the shoulder and tooted. The car had vents on each side like the gills on a shark.

"Oh hell," Tim groaned. "Is that somebody's dad?"

We jogged over, and the passenger door swung out, and a man ducked towards us. "Can I give you men a lift?" He was almost my dad's age, but had a mustache and short hair crowned with a medallion of naked skin. He wore an alligator shirt. Tim and I glanced at each other. Cool air poured out at us.

"Thanks," Tim said as he opened the back door and slid in, obliging me to sit up front. The man wiped a stack of mail from the passenger seat as I got in, then checked the rearview and spun out onto the road. He smelled clean, alcohol-sweet, in the manner of wealthy men. "Where headed?" he asked.

"Ferguson House" I said.

"Really?" His gaze swung to me, then matched itself politely to his profile again. He named two of the boys at Ferguson House, asked if we knew them.

"We've never been there before," Tim said. "We're visiting a friend of a friend."

"I see. Is it summer vacation already?" He said this archly, showed teeth under the mustache.

"We got suspended for fighting," Tim said.

"I noticed your buddy's shiner," said the man. "Which school?" He pressed the cigarette lighter in.

"Bible Baptist," I lied. I unpinned an envelope that was working itself under me.

"I knew it," he said. "I went there when I was y'all's age. You wear the wrong necktie and those people think you're possessed by the devil." He took a pack of thin cigars from the dashboard, shook a filtertip out, and extracted it with his teeth. "Anybody care for a smoke?" The lighter sprang up and he touched it to the little cigar.

"We're scared of cancer," Tim said.

The man said, "It's important to be naughty once in a while."

123

His gaze drifted to me again, and I grew uncomfortably aware of my own body. I studied the mail between us. The top envelope was from a sweepstakes. Another came from a hunting lodge in North Carolina. Both were addressed to Richard Poythress.

The man punched a button and the radio thumped on, and some quiet classical music blended pleasantly with the air conditioning. "I'm Ted," he said. He smiled. "You boys have names?"

"Eric," said Tim.

"Shawn," I said. I started memorizing the name and address on the envelopes.

"I'll bet you boys like to drink, don't you?"

Tim said he liked Cokes a lot. The man said he meant real drinks. We were quiet. The man smoked. The car paused at a four-way stop, the turnoff to the boys' home. Ted-Richard said, "That's a Picasso on your shirt, right?"

Tim said, "Yes, sir."

Ted-Richard drove on without turning. "I drew just like that when I was three years old." He chuckled. I glanced back nervously. Tim was looking at me, forehead grooved.

Tim said, "We missed the turnoff, Ted."

"I decided to invite y'all over for a drink. I've got a swimming pool."

Tim said, "We don't have our bathing suits."

"What the hell," the man said.

I tried to keep breathing evenly. The man said maybe he could loan us swimsuits. Tim and I traded looks again and a sort of telepathic plan to jump out at the next stop.

Ted-Richard said, "Have ya'll ever seen a real polar bear? I've got one mounted in my den. I've also got some Super-8 movies that are hard to get ahold of. They'll make your eyes pop out."

I said, "My dad'll be looking for us at Ferguson House soon."

"Uh-hunh. Now how come he didn't drive you out there, then?"

"He's at work. He'll pick us up on his lunch hour. He's a state patrol officer."

124

"Does he know you hitchhike?" Ted-Richard's smile sharpened beneath the whiskers. "Come on, you boys are pulling my leg, aren't you? If you don't want to go for a swim, maybe we should swing by your school and see if we can straighten things out?"

Tim was looking from me to the man to the shoulder of the road passing beside us at fifty miles an hour, then back again, and I was afraid he might try to leap out.

"I guess you can let us out right here, Mr. Poythress," I said. "I know where your house is, if we feel like stopping by on the way back."

Hearing his name, the man loosened his hold on the steering wheel and smiled with his mouth shut, then dragged on the little cigar. His movements became relaxed, like someone amused and ironical in defeat. The big Lincoln drifted over to the shoulder. We got out into the steamy heat and the car glided away.

"Good move, man," Tim said. "I thought I was going to have to pull my knife on him."

We hiked to a clearing on private land near the orphanage. We squatted against a split-rail fence around a pigsty and waited for the orphan drug dealer, while smallish pigs snuffled in the pen or shaded themselves under the shell of an old truck. In the shack beside it, a TV blared out lunchtime romance. A cat coiled itself tighter on the porch.

A big kid stomped out of the woods and flipped a cigarette butt into a patch of dry grass. I disliked him on sight. He had a training mustache and a hickey the size of a crabapple on his throat.

"Y'all got the money?" He addressed me because I was taller, and I felt embarrassed for Tim. He opened his mouth and stroked the little hairs alongside it.

125

"Yeah," said Tim, rising into his Picasso-at-the-beach stance, chest bullfrogged, arms wide. "You got the illegal substance?"

The boy squinted as if Tim had spoken French. Tim flashed me the face that meant everybody in the world except us was a moron. Tim pulled out five dollars.

The boy took the bills and folded each one separately. He tugged a chain on his belt and a leather wallet hopped out of his seat pocket and swung. He made a ritual of snapping the wallet open, nestling the money inside, and removing a tiny, heat-sealed corner of a plastic bag filled with something like sand. He gave it to Tim.

Tim said, "Rusty says 'Hey.'"

The boy looked over our heads toward the shack, then checked the watch on his leather wristband. "Y'all want to smoke a roach?"

Tim shrugged. The boy fished a squashed cigarette pack from his boot and shook out a charred, home-rolled stub. He lit it and sucked noisily, then took several sharp breaths as he passed it to Tim. Sternly, Tim imitated the boy's method.

I'd had marijuana twice before, inspired by the drug-abuse propaganda films at school, but had never achieved a high from it. I worried it had ruined my chromosomes, though.

Tim gave me the little cigarette, coughing through his nose. The boy peered over our heads again. I resolved that as long as I was stripping my genes, I might as well try for the full effect. I took a mighty drag, and it flared and crackled. My throat burned, and I coughed, mouth clamped, white puffs bursting from my nostrils. The boy smirked and took the joint, licked it to slow the burning. I decided I'd wipe it off next time.

Tim inhaled some, coughed, smeared tears from his eyes. "You know this is the same crap they make rope out of?"

The boy produced an electrical clip and pinched the last of the joint in it, and we sucked at it until it vanished. The final puff left me hacking. The orphan's eyes were dark and shiny now, cracked with red. He grinned. The purplish blotch on his neck seemed more hideous as I imagined how he'd acquired it.

"Are you sure that was real pot?" Tim asked. He made a horrendous noise and hawked a comet of phlegm towards the trees.

"Don't wrestle with it," said the boy. "Let it take you off, like falling asleep."

I began to notice things differently. After a numb minute Tim said, "Hey, man, does it bother you not to have parents?"

"Fuck no," the boy said. Then he was still for a while and his features began to twitch. "Fuck yeah," he said.

There was a squeal and a bang, like a pig had been shot, and my heart detonated. I whipped around. It hadn't been a shot at all, but a screendoor creaking open, slamming shut. An obese woman stood on the porch of the house. All the pigs trotted over, unharmed, and pressed up to the fence on that side. The boy said, "Later," and went towards her. She hardly bothered to look at us. She wore an inadequate halter-top and too much green eyeshadow, but I felt an intense and troubling desire for her. I guessed the drug had me. The woman slid her hand in the boy's back pocket, and they went inside.

The weed's effect was strong, but not extraordinary if you'd had it before. We had no precedent, though, and so it was a plunge into the rabbit's hole.

Everything glowed. My heart kept thundering, and I still seemed to feel there'd been a pig-shooting. Invisible claws gripped my shoulders. I was afraid Richard Poythress was after us. Tim looked at me with what seemed horror, and then I saw his face in different ways, as if I were many people seeing him for the first time, noticing one feature then another, instead of the shorthand way I was accustomed to. Beneath this was the recollection that God didn't exist, nothing could save us.

"Damn," Tim said. "Why'd we smoke that stuff? We don't know what was in it—"

I advised myself to relax, exhaled hundreds of pounds of

anxiety, then heard the hurricane inrush of my breath and felt it swell my belly. Distances lengthened, distances collapsed. Objects acquired a curvy shine like balloon sculpture. I chuckled. Tim winced.

"Oh, man . . ." I said or thought.

"So I'm small," Tim said. "Stop staring at me."

"What?" I said. "Did you . . . ?"

We giggled. The sky burned neon blue. Tim sniffed his fingers. My neck tickled and I rubbed it, something crumbling moistly.

"Look at this swarm of bugs," Tim said in slow motion. He was rolling his face around like an aborigine in Disney World. "Where'd they come from?"

The air was flickering with tiny white wings. A flying ant floated onto the hair of my arm. They drifted everywhere, lit all over me, and I brushed them off gently or blew on them until they flew away. I itched all over, but it passed.

Tim fanned the air in front of his face, saying, "Goddamnit, I think I inhaled one."

I sat. Soft grass blades slipped between my fingers, and a drowsy wind breathed pine and nectar over me. I thought of Margie, recalled that I was spending the night with her, and had a physical reaction while seeming to believe back-and-forth that she was and wasn't with us now. Images of Margie and Donny writhing on each other in bed now filled me with a strange lust. Insects snowed around us in crystalline sunlight.

Tim pointed to a palmetto nearby. "Something jumped."

Again, a frond jerked, and I heard a tap. I stared until I saw a green lizard on the green palmetto, chewing.

Chameleons appeared in the landscape, some standing on their hindlegs. They sprang from perch to perch, catching the insects in their almond mouths. They chewed, stalked the next bug. I watched a green lizard turn brown.

A redbird hopped along the fencetop, pecking insects out of the air, feasting. From the house, the cat slunk over and crouched by a tree, and a lizard streaked up the trunk. The cat flattened into the grass, ears back, flying ants collecting on its fur.

"This is like one of those food-chain diagrams we studied," I said. "And I'm kind of hungry too."

"I can't bear to watch that cat kill anything," Tim said. "Let's book before that hoodlum gets back."

We stood up. The boy's cigarette butt had scorched a sort of totem-face into the grass, and it grinned at me with glowing teeth. I ground the sparks out with my sneaker, imagining myself an initiate in some primitive, magical tribe.

A Test of the Emergency Broadcast System

The afternoon was slow and mysterious. My consciousness, due to the pot, was a bundle of telescopes: I'd start seeing through one of them and forget the others, then I'd recall them and my mind would shift, slide down another tube, and get trapped there a while, enlarging the details at the end. Sometimes I felt normal, then immediately I'd feel warped.

We dozed on a bus most of the way back to town. I said good-bye to Tim outside of Blessed Heart, four hundred inside voices murmuring "Praise to You, Lord Jesus Christ," as the school suffered our weekly Mass. Tim crept into the vestibule to consult the list of forbidden movies, condemned by the U.S. Catholic Conference. He convinced his parents to take him to those.

Safely home, I ate snacks and leftovers in a sequence that made me nauseated, then took a nap. It seemed I never fell asleep, but I remembered odd dreams. I went and collected Peter from school and deposited him in front of the TV with John. When Mama got home, I asked if I could spend the weekend at Tim's.

"Your daddy and I are going to a party there tonight. Why do you need to sleep over two nights?" She moved into the kitchen, lifted the phone receiver.

"Tonight's for drawing, tomorrow's for camping out," I said.

"Francis, I won't inflict you on the Sullivans two nights in a row." Her hands, phone included, went to her hips.

"They invited me."

In the living room the television was blank and whining, a test of the Emergency Broadcast System. My true purpose—staying the night with Margie—made me so desperate that real anguish tore my voice. I suggested that my artistic and outdoors pursuits were healthy, whereas beating your children bloody was something you didn't want the neighbors to hear about.

I was ashamed of myself for this, of course, but I saw it working on her. She patted the receiver on her thigh. I stared forlornly at the kitchen tiles, their obsolete space-age pattern. Mama countered with her drunken-stepfather-and-his-razor-strop anecdote, then set the price: "Clean your room, wash the dog, do the dishes."

She began an hour on the phone. The Emergency Broadcast System test was followed by a cartoon cat chasing a cartoon mouse with an axe.

I glossed my room by shaking the wrinkles out of the bedspreads on each bunk, then organizing all the knickknacks (shark's teeth, arrowheads) into symmetrical patterns wherever they lay. I crammed games and sports equipment and toys into the closet and under the beds.

Bathing Gretchen, the dachshund, was quick, though I had to hoist her, squirming, back into the tub four times, then swab the floor with towels.

Because my mother was only a dilettante at housework, washing the dishes was a monumental chore. I tied an apron on.

The automatic dishwasher promises ease, but it lies. It was

half full from its previous use. I unloaded it into cabinets and drawers, heedless of grease spots or dried-on food. Then I began to dismantle the teetering dish-pyramids in the sink, reliving various meals as I ran each item through a scalding cylinder of water. I scraped petrified spaghetti from five plates and a pot, while the neighborhood kids laughed and shrieked at their outside games. The sun sagged into the top of the window over the sink. I shaved coagulated lard from a frying pan. The sink filled with a reddish soup, and a mummified fly rose and floated.

The sun centered itself in the window, branding circles into my eyes. I fetched my mirror sunglasses, put them on. I stuffed the dishwasher beyond its abilities, knowing the plastic items would flip and fill with greasy water, or fly loose and melt.

The dishwasher wouldn't close until I pried a pitcher out, washed it by hand.

Four messy plates remained in the sink. I cleaned one, squirting soap onto it, scraping off the food-rocks with my softening fingernails, then rinsed it, dried it, and stacked it away. This consumed the span of an entire "Looney Tune," which I heard my brothers howling at.

With pale, wrinkled hands, I attached the dishwasher to the faucet, clicked the dial to Heavy Load, and the machine hissed and strained and thumped. I gathered the last dirty plates, stepped out into the lane, and sailed them like Frisbees, ceramic exploding on gravel. The past two weeks had worked me into an end-of-the-world point of view where nothing would be left after Sunday, and I wasn't going to waste another moment.

I stepped back inside as Daddy, trailing the odor of dead chickens from work, lifted a beer from the refrigerator. I stood before him in my apron and sunglasses.

"What the hell are you supposed to be?"

"Blinded in the line of duty," I said and groped past him towards the doorway, eyes closed behind the dark lenses.

132

"Just wait till The Service gets ahold of you, son."

I showered, washing all of it twice.

I entered the wilderness of Tim's backyard and heard a ticking through the curtains of greenery near the clubhouse. I waded the waist-high grass, carrying my duffel bag overhead.

"One more step, Francis, and you'll have an unusual experience." Tim had a blowgun at his lips, a long camouflaged tube with a mouthpiece. He'd bought it last year from a comic-book ad.

Beside me, propped against the clubhouse, was a painted plywood cutout of President Nixon, his chest bristling with darts. I stepped back. Tim's cheeks bulbed, he huffed, and a dart flicked shivering into Nixon's heart.

"I've been practicing," Tim said as I walked to him. "The marijuana actually seemed to help. You have to perceive yourself, the blowgun, the dart, and the target as all parts of the same thing." He drew a dart from the quiver, a swatch of foam rubber around the blowgun's shaft. The dart was six inches of pointed wire joined to a plastic yellow cone for propulsion. This dart was odd, its stem fattened with a brown crust.

"This is one of our wildcat tranquilizers," Tim explained. "I cooked up a paste of the angel dust and dabbed it onto the wire, then blow-dried it." He had left the tip bare so we wouldn't get drugged if it pricked us by accident. He grinned.

In a TV character voice I said, "Thank heavens you're using your powers for the forces of Good."

Tim was able to laugh and spit cleanly at the same time.

✝

"That black eye makes you look sort of 'two-fisted,' Francis," said Mrs. Sullivan, Tim's mother. "Your parents are coming tonight, I hope?"

Mrs. Sullivan's dress was low-cut and blooming with candy-colored flowers, her hair in honey-butter curls. She had skewered her earlobes with golden hoops. She wore lipstick, mascara, Indian beads. My mental scrapbook showed Mrs. Sullivan in glasses, cutoffs, and a sweat shirt, hair French-braided. Even smart women will turn themselves into a confection for their guests.

"I'm not batting my lashes at you," she said and patted my chest. "It's these damn contact lenses."

I said the things you say to nice mothers, affected a boyish politeness which was close to real, and carried my duffel bag into Tim's room.

Tim bolted us in, slapped a finger across his cassette player, and Alice Cooper began sneering "School's Out" from several small, naked speakers wired throughout the room. One wall was all bookshelves, and books were stacked everywhere else too. Another wall featured surrealist, impressionist, and comic-book art posters.

Tim raked some fanzines and comics out of the way so we could sit on the bed. His drawing table offered the only bare space in the room. The rest was a metropolis of monster models, chemistry sets, Tim's paintings and constructions, weaponry, magic kits.

Tim said, "You'd better hang around until your parents see that you're actually here."

"Yeah, I figured that out for myself."

"Fine. We'll get juiced meantime. Or I will. They say firewater interferes with the act of love. I have no way of knowing, of course."

"It doesn't seem to affect me much," I said. "I have to keep my hands in my pockets, to cover, even when I just talk to her. I'm afraid not to drink."

"I'm almost tempted to stay sober for this party. Watching these professors and rich people is like going to the zoo. I told you I walked in on a couple screwing in my bed one night. They messed up half a dozen magazines."

Tim handed me William Blake's *Songs of Experience,* told me to read "The Tiger," and left to get us drinks. The doorbell rang. Rang again. The poem was simple and strange and made my arm-hair rise.

Tim returned with two Cokes, gave me one. The doorbell continued.

"Easy, man," Tim said. "That's about 40 percent rum."

When the Alice Cooper tape clicked off, jazz breezed in from the living room, along with the rolling laughter of conversations and the chiming of ice in glass. Tim fed an Elton John tape into his multiphonic player. We read and drank for about an hour. We tried to make a threatening phone call to Richard Poythress, friend of young boys, but his number was unlisted and the operator proved untrickable. The doorbell ringings grew infrequent. Tim asked if I thought my parents were here by now. I said probably.

"Let's stiffen these Cokes and go catch the antics in the other rooms," he said. "Then you can rendezvous with the dream girl."

The living room smelled like a volcano, made my eyes sting. Ashtrays and lost drinks gathered in the low places. A woman I knew looked at me and said, "What's a nice boy like you . . . ?" and laughed hoarsely, heaving her bust up into the scoop of her sweater. I glimpsed rosy flesh near the tip of a breast, my stomach tightening. She went to school with my mom. Rode a motorcycle.

My parents stood in the territory between living room and dining room. Mama's gown displayed most of her back, which embarrassed me, and Daddy wore Sansabelt slacks, a checkered shirt, and a wide tie, also embarrassing. A sweaty man gestured comically in front of them, only occasionally bothering to glance at my dad, then went limp and guffawed, potbelly heaving, and they laughed too. Dad slurped beer right from the can.

"Don't act so ashamed," Tim said. "They're the least bullshitty couple here."

Mama saw me, and her hand went up like a butterfly. Daddy smiled. The man gaped at me.

Tim's father was sitting in his leather recliner, sipping from a shot glass. He had a beard and pink indentations on each side of his nose bridge. He wore a dashiki. A man yammered to him about the Gods From Outer Space theory. Mr. Sullivan saw us, winked hello, and killed us with his gun finger. "Did you hellions get to see the flying ant invasion?"

"During recess," Tim said. "Cute shirt, Dad." Frowning, he guided me into the kitchen. "Time for more medication." He topped off our bottles with rum, in plain sight of the sweaty man who'd been laughing with my folks.

"Shit, Timmy," the man said, "at least pretend like you think I'm an adult." The man's shirt was damp at the throat, the breastbone, beneath the armpits and pectorals, and in a stripe down his belly that flared out at his navel. He breathed loudly. He clawed ice cubes from a silver bucket, dropped them into his glass, added vodka. He was leering into the living room. "Will you look at the lungs on that chick?"

The motorcycle woman had wiggled into my dad's lap when he sat on the couch. She was bent over so that her breasts hung down against the sweater and created a thick slice of cleavage.

Daddy, smirking, sipped beer as if this was everyday. His hair was fluffed on one side, his nose lit up.

"I've got your husband, Jackie!" the woman roared at my mom.

"That's your problem!" shouted Mama, and people laughed.

The sweaty man tipped vodka into his mouth, then spat ice back into the glass. He wiped his lip and grinned. "Shit, I figure she'll stumble into my lap next, only I ain't letting her get away. She's just what this fat drunk boy ordered. Is that your mama standing over there, son?"

"Yes," I said. "Sir."

"She's pretty. Are you adopted? Just kidding. Hey, I'm overdue for a piss." He plodded through the rooms, turned his glass up over his mouth, throat pumping, and smacked his shoulder on the door jamb going into the hallway.

"Attorney," Tim said. "People pay that jack-off thousands of dollars to escape punishment for their crimes."

Mrs. Sullivan glided around the furniture, sliding coasters under drinks, pushing trays of miniature food at people. My own mother's laugh, high and syrupy, cut through the others. She was smiling as if the entire planet was delightful, eyes gone Oriental, touching everyone near her. I was glad I wouldn't be home tomorrow when she and Daddy suffered "sinus headaches" and stationed a bucket beside the bed.

"I'm ready to be away from here," I said

We lowered ourselves out of the window in Tim's room. Tim accomplished this with a Coke bottle clamped in his teeth.

A floodlight ignited the backyard into a surreal jungle, Day-Glo leaves splashed on rippling black velvet. Tim swayed, guzzled from the bottle.

"Watch," he said. "I'm the famous painter Jackson Pollock." He took a mouthful of rum Coke and spewed it on the whitewashed side of his house, tossing his head and bobbing. A caramel-colored mess spread and dripped. "Still Life with Drool."

He finished laughing at himself, turned to me sloppily, and asked if I'd bathed and brushed my teeth.

"Are you supposed to be my trainer?"

"Sorry. I guess I'm excited for you. Here's a gift." He turned his pocket inside out, getting a small, square packet, and tossed it to me. "Prophylactic. That's a rubber to you. Lubricated and tropical green. I've had it a while, but I know I'll never get a chance to use it."

I'd been so tense about sleeping over at Margie's that I'd convinced myself nothing dramatic was going to happen. I respected her too much. She was still upset because I'd told her secret. She wouldn't want to get involved in sex for a long time, after what had happened. But Tim made it seem like I was expected to go all the way with her, and I got scared all over again.

"Look," Tim said, "I'm sorry about letting the cat out of the bag about you-know-what. Tell her I'm sorry, I'm just a frustrated dwarf. I hope your hernia doesn't cause any problems."

My stomach was full of wasps now. "Wait a minute, maybe I need to plan this out more," I said.

"Don't turn chicken. You've got to live dangerously. You have nothing to fear but fear itself—of impotence and VD and premature—"

I entered the leaves.

"Electric light's a miracle," Tim slurred.

I stopped, turned. "Hunh?"

He snickered. "Well, I just mean it's wonderful, if you look at it with Martian eyes. If you pretend you're seeing it for the first time. See? Never mind."

I heard him gulping, then his bottle thwacked off the club-house. He belched three times, each burp more ragged than the one before. "I've learned how to burp!" he said. "I've discovered the secret of burping."

The light through the leaves was like hundreds of new quarters being flung into the blackness. It blinked on my eyelashes as I turned to go.

I bought gum and stole a bottle of Boone's Farm Strawberry Hill wine. I combed my hair on the way to Margie's, unable to generate entire thoughts. I began to talk to myself like an air-traffic controller comforting the pilot of a crippled plane. Be calm. You can make it, buddy. We're standing by.

I halted on the sidewalk outside of the Flynns' enormous house. I hung my head, found I was standing in a hopscotch rectangle chalked onto the pavement. I felt dreadfully ill and ashamed of my fear and would've rather taken a whipping than go into that house. I looked up for the stars, in order to see all of this in its true insignificance. Above me, a rat ran along a trembling telephone wire. I broke a sweat.

Margie's silhouette appeared in an upstairs window, waved and vanished, and then the front door opened, sent light across the porch. I staggered towards it.

Margie shouted, "Peaches! No!"

I didn't see the dog until it had my shin in its jaws, snarling like a chain saw, jerking me across the lawn.

Welcome to
Horrible Movies

I sat on the bed beside a stuffed bear while Margie, kneeling in a miniskirt, daubed rubbing alcohol onto the teeth holes in my ankle. It felt similar to a jellyfish stinging. In sympathy, Margie supplied the noises I was stifling, little backward hisses at each touch of the Kleenex. I distracted myself by studying the stripe of pale bare skin where her short, sleeveless top ended and the skirt began. She had on high heels.

"She's a strong dog," I said, "for her size."

"Patrick's supposed to lock her in the yard at night, but Mama wasn't here to make him. I should've thought of it." She tipped some alcohol onto the tissue. "This'll hurt."

She pressed the Kleenex to the deepest bite. We both flinched and my knee flew up beside her face. The dog howled in the backyard. As Margie patched my leg with Band-Aids, it occurred to me how deliberate things were. We hadn't seen any of her brothers on the way up, though now I heard the murmurings of boys and television. Smoke was drifting up from a stick of incense in a nearby potted fern. Margie's eyes, cheeks, and lips were made up, and her hair had been tamed out of her eyes by a turquoise barrette.

Her arms, legs, and middle were very bare, and she radiated

gusts of perfume that smelled moist, like a misted flower garden. I didn't feel worthy of all this.

Margie's room had been built into the attic, and one wall was really the roof slanting down over the bed, the paneling brightened with posters. Disney's *Alice in Wonderland* and some black-light psychedelics. A plastic rainbow curved above the headboard and a silk daisy hung its head from an elongated 7UP bottle on the night table.

Downstairs, the TV announced the defeat of our local baseball team, and one of the brothers swore.

Margie stood up, tugged the miniskirt smooth, and clicked on her stereo, a more elaborate machine than my parents could afford. A bleak piano began to plink, and Harry Nilsson sang that he couldn't live, if livin was without you, then howled it in harmony with his own multiplied voice.

I said, "That's one of my favorite songs."

She said, "Mine too."

I glanced at the photographs tucked into the frame of the mirror on a white wicker vanity, mostly shots of Margie and horses. An old group photo of a Brownie troop. One teenage male pop singer, barechested. Margie saw me looking and snatched the heartthrob from the glass and wadded him into a wicker basket. "My mom gave me that," she explained, true pink blooming around her rouge. "I had to keep it a while."

I still had the Boone's Farm Strawberry Hill wine in my hand. "Want to drink some of this?" I said. "It's pretty good."

"Okay. Or we could try some champagne first." Her eyes scanned the room. "If you want."

I guessed it was part of the plan. "Sure, whatever you want."

"Don't go anywhere." She laid her hand on my shoulder, kissed my bruised eye, then rather awkwardly yanked off her heels and exchanged them in the closet for a pair of flat red shoes, smiled like she was embarrassed again, and left. I thought this must be how it felt to be married.

In a minute she was back with a bottle of Andre and a Siamese cat winding between her feet.

"Let me open it," I said, taking the bottle. "I'm good at this." I popped the stopper out the way Daddy had shown me and pressed my palm to the bottle's mouth until the bubbles relaxed, then raised my hand and a pale tongue of carbonation darted out. Margie lifted champagne glasses out of a dresser drawer. I was flattered by all this contrivance, but my anxiety increased, like an understudy who hears that the leading man's had an accident, and that now everything's up to him.

"You're positive your mother's not coming home?" I asked. The bottle kept ringing against the glasses as I poured.

"Uh huh. But it wouldn't matter. She wouldn't come up here." Margie handed me my glass, sat beside me. The Siamese hopped onto the bed and mewed loudly, frequently. Her body was cream colored and she had a chocolate-dipped face, tail, and legs, and an idiot's blue eyes.

We each sipped a glassful of champagne, then agreed to move on to the wine, which looked to be sweeter. The label said, "Serve Very Cold," but it was lukewarm. I cracked the screw top, it fizzled, a glitter of bubbles rising, and then I took a long instinctive pull before I remembered I was supposed to be sharing it with a girl prior to romance, not bolstering myself against an ordeal.

Margie and I drank in the traditional Boone's Farm way, passing the bottle between us. She smiled and said, "MMm," and treated me to the green of her eyes. Our fingers touched on purpose, driving my blood faster.

The dog attack and the drinking had cleared some of my worry so that lust could sneak back in. Margie's bare midriff tempted me. I inhaled her perfume aura. "You sure smell good," I said.

"Thanks." She crooked her wrist under her nose, sniffed. "I

142

think I might've put on too much perfume." She offered me the wrist.

I took her hand, inhaled more of the drizzly fragrance, and kissed the whitish scar across the cords of her wrist. She didn't pull her arm back. I kissed again.

From downstairs Donny yelled, "Margie!" She slumped and rolled her eyes, then recovered, but for that moment she looked extremely young.

At other times I had noted, and dismissed, the slight crookedness of Margie's nose, the vaccination dimple at her shoulder, a pink mole on her throat. I saw them now, again, and regretted that she wasn't perfect, although she was so nearly perfect that it frightened me. Then I was able to ignore them again, aided by the alcohol.

My denim-covered thigh touched her bare one, magnetized towards the heat, and our little fingers found each other and tangled like mating snakes. She turned her mouth up to me, and I kissed her without pressure, drank some wine, kissed her deeply, and then instead of passing her the bottle I poured my mouth full with the magic soda and shared it as we kissed, her mouth grinding eagerly against mine, clicking my teeth, and her delirious breathing made a tight, satisfying pressure in my lap. The cat butted purring against my hip. I touched the bare stripe of Margie's waist, explored around the soft curve, incapable of believing any of this. Perfume, incense, and cheap strawberry flavoring sweetened everything.

I slid my hand inside the back of her shirt and stroked girl-skin, which even on a thin girl is softer than your own. My hand smoothed circles up her back then stalled on the stitched cloth of a bra clasp, and I got timid again because she arched and pressed against me to make it easier for me to unsnap it. The music finished. The stereo ticked, tapped, shut off, and her brothers' voices returned.

143

The condom packet in my pocket felt like a murder weapon. I pictured myself undressed in front of Margie, ugly as a conch peeled from its shell. I wondered if she and Donny had committed incest right here on this bed, and I wilted and began to ache. Margie pulled back, asked what she'd done wrong.

Donny yelled up, "Margie! Where's the can of spaghetti?"

She turned angrily to the door and yelled, "I cooked it! Make something else!"

"Maybe Doyle's hungry too!"

Donny's knowing that I was there caused me to feel guilty and criminal. I checked for an alternate escape route, but there was only the wisteria-veined window, stopped up with an air conditioner. Margie jumped up and slammed the door, turned to me with a smile, and asked if maybe I was hungry.

"Just thirsty," I said.

"Well, let's talk then, and drink."

I assumed she was being patient with my bashfulness, and I was grateful, but I also felt like she was in control. She lifted the cat and sat in the chair across from me, our knees a knife blade's width apart, and the cat narrowed its crossed eyes in delight at each stroke she gave it.

"So," she drawled, "what're you doing tomorrow that's so top-secret?"

I told her how the bobcat was supposed to free us all from Blessed Heart, distract Father Kavanagh from our filthy comic book, and provide the gang with its final adventure.

"That's pretty neat," she said. "But you better not get hurt. Did your friend Tim come up with this plan?"

I admitted he had.

"Well you just better be careful. He's crazy. I can recognize crazy people, you know." She had affected a pout, very cute and persuasive. It made me want to put my hands on her.

"You remind me of Tim in certain ways," I said. "I bet you two would get along real well." I wished I hadn't said that,

144

because Tim seemed much more attractive than me, and was approximately Margie's height.

"No," she said, the pout reversing into a smile, teasing. "He's a maniac. I only get along with you."

Through the door we heard Donny yell, "Margie! Where the fuck is the motherfucking can opener?"

"Ignore him," Margie said. "He's the biggest baby." She plucked the wine bottle from my lap and drank some, then asked if I wanted to watch "Horrible Movies," the local Friday night monster film. I'd always considered that show my particular property. Sharing it seemed safely intimate, so I said fine. She turned off the lights and turned on the small color set atop her chest of drawers. I could tell by the way her steps thumped the floor that she was not used to drinking this much.

"Horrible Movies" was the reward I looked forward to each week of my childhood. It appeared in the mysterious hours beyond my parents' bedtime, in the democratic black-and-white which was just as good on our old set as any new one. I loved being entertained by the dead, Karloff or Lugosi, or the unknowns who seemed like real people. These movies renewed the world with strangeness, in the way the denatured magic of religion failed to do, werewolves and living dead testifying to other realities, the importance of the invisible. They made you suffer pursuit, dungeons, tombs, and afterwards you surrendered consciousness, received nightmares, and Sunday morning you rose, still alive, stronger by one more horror.

Margie and I snuggled on her bed against pillows and stuffed animals, and I was almost numb enough, at first, to feel comfortable with her head on my chest, her careless blonde curls tickling my chin. I willed my heart to slowness beneath her ear.

After an eccentric used car commercial and some public service announcements, the TV darkened amid the minor chord spiralings and rumble of Bach's Toccata and Fugue, and host Robin Graves materialized, wearing an executioner's robe, photographed in negative against a graveyard backdrop. "Welcome to . . . 'Horrible . . . Moo-vies' . . ." he said in a deep burbling, electronic voice. He joked morbidly, then announced tonight's feature, *The Cat People*. Margie began hiccupping. She held her breath.

The TV flicked to black-and-white, green at the edges. The movie was about a young woman, an immigrant from the Old Country, who believed she had a curse that changed her into a panther when she was angry or jealous or kissed a man. I had a hard time following it, because I wasn't used to having a beautiful girl up against me. She stopped hiccupping.

As it grew later, the commercials dwindled and the story began to seem real, and it got creepy. Margie and I kept exchanging drunken glances in the jumping glow, seeing ourselves in the characters, the same as you sometimes believe a song on the radio is meant especially for you. After a scare that made even me jump, Margie clenched a wad of my shirt in each fist and tugged with every stab of music or ominous close-up, shutting her eyes against the worst moments. Robin Graves returned and made fun of the movie, but Margie was still stiff against me.

Later the Cat Woman's rival went swimming in an indoor pool at night, water reflections slicing at the walls and ceiling. The panther crept in and paced the lip of the pool as the woman paddled, panicking, in the deep center of the pool. Margie began crying against me, and the movie shrank into the distant box of the TV.

"I'm sorry," she whispered. "Can you please turn it off? I can't stand to watch anything scary right now, because of my nerves."

I didn't want to stop the movie. I wanted the mystery solved, and also the TV was like a third person in the room who lessened my duty towards Margie. But I rolled off the bed and extinguished it, the tiny fading eye of the picture dying in a blink. I flipped on the light.

Margie was curled on the bed with her eyes squeezed shut

and her arms around herself, whispering, "I'm so awful," with tears tracking unaccustomed mascara down her face.

I touched her back and said, "Margie, it's off. What's wrong?"

"Everything's horrible." Her voice was high and tiny like a small child's, and slurred from the wine. "It feels like the eyes of the posters are watching me, even though I know that's stupid. I just feel scared." She swallowed and looked up at me with her eyes filling and lips trembling, and I felt coldhearted for noticing that her earrings and teardrops flashed with the same exact sparkle. She said, "You think I lied about the ghost to get you up here with me, don't you? But I didn't. Either she's real, or I'm crazy."

Margie was shivering now, and had the hiccups again. I hadn't even thought about the ghost once. I said, of course, "You're not crazy."

"Well, I'm so scared of being crazy," she hiccupped, "that I'm going crazy from worrying."

"Well it doesn't worry me. Be crazy if you want. Just relax."

She sank into the corner of the bed against the slanted wall and the headboard and watched herself across in the mirror as if it was someone dangerous. I didn't entirely understand and wasn't sure how to involve myself. Maybe I should go home and leave her alone, I thought, since I wasn't helping. I lifted the wine bottle and drank what was left, then started into the champagne, though I'd begun seeing two of everything and sensed nausea behind the deadened wall of myself. Still afraid to go to bed with her, I figured drunkenness was the least sissy way to avoid it.

Margie said, "I know you feel weird around me. I'm bad and horrible." Tears leapt from her lashes. "Everybody hates Donny and thinks he's the bad one. But I made him do it to me." She wept at the mirror, hiccupping. "I tricked him one night when he was stoned, and then I blackmailed him into doing it all the time. And I loved it, it's all I thought about. I'm much, much

147

worse than him, and I don't see how you can stand me." She dropped her head, sobbing in a whisper.

I'd already digested the softer version of this that she'd told me in the park, and like my hernia, my brother's brain damage, and the knowledge that death is the world's landlord, I'd begun to live with it. But she refused to forgive herself.

She continued to hiccup, and her face was smeared with mascara. "You know, I used to sit alone in my room every day doing nothing, thinking awful things. I felt like I was the only true person in the world, like everybody else was a robot put here to test me."

"I've felt like that before," I said. "Have you been to a psychiatrist?"

"They made me go. All the doctor did was ask me questions about the divorce and all. He kept telling me I was normal, which is bullshit. And he gave me pills that made me feel dumb and sleepy."

"Maybe you were just caught up in your own imagination. I got the idea, one time, that I had stomach cancer. And worrying about it made my stomach hurt more. For six months I believed I had cancer, then I got my hernia and worried about that instead." I felt I was so drunk I wasn't making sense. She didn't seem to be listening.

"When I couldn't get Donny in here—" She hiccupped again and the crying got worse, "—I'd use my fingers and think about him or some other boy. Or my dad . . . sometimes worse stuff . . ." She knocked the back of her skull against the wall. "God! I'm so messed up!"

She got up and lurched over to the mirror and sat down hard in the chair. She stopped crying, put out her finger, and touched her mirror finger. "I think I look ugly and awful. I don't know why you came here."

"You don't have to tell me all this stuff," I said. "If everybody did everything that came into their heads, we'd all be waiting on the electric chair."

She stared into the mirror, and seemed to me very self-consciously dramatic, like she was doing something she'd seen in a movie. I realized that she was so locked up in herself that everything she did seemed important, that her crimes were too big ever to be forgiven. I was a little angry by then, and so drunk I couldn't sit straight, but I drank the champagne down to the bottom. I thought if I ignored her now she might remember I existed. I braced on the mattress and stared at the rolling carpet. I heard a whack and the cat shot between my feet under the bed.

Margie was pounding the mirror with open hands. I stumbled over, grabbed her wrists where the razor scars were. She made fists and strained groaning towards the glass and said, "Don't touch me!" I looked at her face in the mirror and was startled at my own image.

I've always encountered myself as a stranger, an unfamiliar boy in photographs, reflections. It's not the same me I recognize in dreams. I knew I didn't like this boy either, I couldn't even stand the way he looked, drunk and dopey and standing around while this little girl indulged in hysterics. I let go of Margie's wrists and she smacked the glass hard, and a crack ran from one corner to its diagonal opposite.

What I did next began as an accident. I thought it, and then I was doing it before I could stop. I punched my mirror face. Pieces fell on the vanity table, a noise that made me angrier, enraged at my own violent stupidity. Margie gasped. The boy didn't vanish, he scattered into fragments, and I punched the mirror again and again, the same animal rhythm my father used when he beat me, a sick crashing ecstasy with the glass all falling, Margie tugging back on my waist, until I was thudding wood, leaving dull bloodstains. I swung my elbow and the mirror frame jumped cracking against the wall.

You can't kill your reflection. Each shard contained another version.

I felt that the door had opened behind me. Donny was framed there in an attitude of shock, but still chewing something, his arm in a fresh white cast. Margie was half on the floor, attached to my waist, a seductress clinging to her barbarian on the cover of a pulp novel. Donny swallowed hugely, like a python, and said, "I heard a noise up here. Are y'all okay?" then fastened his eyes on mine as I nodded feebly and the pain came into my hands. Donny turned and closed the door behind him with great politeness.

My mind still smoking, I slid nicked fingers through Margie's hair. My knuckles were cut, not badly. "Son of a bitch," I said. "Feel any better now?" Somehow I did.

She said, "In a way, I guess. I think you stopped my hiccups."

I offered to pay for the damage, having only about three dollars in the world. She said not to worry about it, that I should see her brothers' rooms.

Several hushed male voices deliberated in the hall below the stairway. It was important to me that no older boys come in, pseudo-parents who might reduce me to a drunken kid helping a disturbed little girl destroy furniture. I didn't want to hear this was silly, or I'd better go home now, or that I was in more trouble. Margie stepped over to the door and dropped the latch in its eyelet.

I got down on the crackling floor (it seemed natural at the time) and sprawled on my back. Margie brushed some shards away with her shoe and got down beside me. I saw there were glow-in-the-dark stars pasted on the ceiling.

"My head is so jumbled up," Margie said.

I nodded my head, as if I understood.

"Don't agree," she pleaded. "Contradict me."

I tried to dredge up some wisdom to apply to this. "You never know what's enough until you know what's more than enough," I said.

Her forehead wrinkled and smoothed, and she breathed evenly. "That sort of makes sense. You mean, it's like all the people who make up the rules to begin with, they're the ones who went too far and know where everybody else ought to stop." She turned towards me, a smile washing up on her face. "You're smart."

"I got that from Tim, who got it from William Blake—a poet who made these religious comic books in the old days."

"Well, that's better than anything the doctor told me."

"He was probably trying to make you regular. Some people need to learn how to be unusual, how to work on the good parts of it and not let the rest worry you. I'm not exactly regular, which is why I like you, even though you're crazy and you're driving me crazy, as you can see." I swept a hand through the air, indicating general destruction.

She giggled, after all of that.

We lay on the carpet, staring at the ceiling. I pushed myself up and slapped the light switch off, then rolled back down and held Margie's hand. The stars on the ceiling glowed pale green. Margie put an arm and a leg across me and, wet with tears, kissed my ear. But I tensed.

"Margie, I really love you." Drunk, this was easy to say. "But I think I'm too, um, messed up to—you know—do anything." I was scared to even give it a name, especially the standard, "make love," which you heard every three minutes on the radio.

"That's okay," she said, removing her arm and leg. "It's probably best, considering what got me into all this mess in the first place." She kissed my cheek and sighed. "Sometimes I feel like I got my life backwards." Then, after a while, "I see colored sparkles in the dark. Can you see them?"

"Yeah." I saw them every night, like private fireworks, even with my eyes closed. "I guess it's just stuff inside our eyes. Rods or cones or whatever."

The cat had reappeared, slinking tentatively around us, and now I felt her tongue on my knuckles, a warm rasp against the drying blood.

"Francis," Margie said, "tell me the most amazing thing you ever heard."

I pondered, then said, "There's this fish that lives at the bottom of the ocean, and it has a spine sticking out of its head with a light at the tip, to lure prey. The females are the glowing ones, the males are smaller. Well—" I almost yawned. "—after the male fish hatch they bite onto a female. They're like parasites. But after a while their bodies grow into each other, and they share the same blood and everything." My skin pinched into goose bumps thinking about this. "They turn into one single fish."

"Wow," said Margie drowsily. "That's really weird."

Our heads were touching, and it seemed like her thoughts were jumping into my brain faster than they could travel to her own heart. I turned my face to her and her mouth was against mine in a very tender kiss that grew warmer, more desperate, her mouth changing from soft to loose and wet and then wide open, tongue hard, her hands squeezing my shoulder and my arm. The hair on my neck tingled. Because I knew we weren't taking this to its adult conclusion, I didn't mind going right up to the edge, peering over, safe against the plunge.

I kissed her and she tilted her head back, offering me her throat, and her breathing quickened whenever I licked or nibbled. She slid her hands down my back, untucked my shirt, and eased one hand up my back and the other into the waistband of my jeans. She was squirming under me now, and I found that I was squirming too. I took tiny bites of her shoulder, and she gasped at my ear and then her tongue slid inside, an odd squishy cave-sound, and every nerve in my body stood up and shivered. We writhed against each other.

"Ow! Stop!" she cried.

"What'd I do?"

"I'm on a piece of glass. Ouch. Let's get on the bed."

We repositioned ourselves and started again. My hands found her bare waist and stroked up under her shirt to her small, cloth-cupped breasts. Her hand wriggled into my underwear, slightly uncomfortable, but I got used to it. I eased my fingers under the bra and discovered her nipples, urgently hard in the soft mounds of her breasts. She leaned up and crooked her arm around and unsnapped her bra, then maneuvered it off her shoulders and out through the sleevehole around one arm, smiling at me like an accomplice.

I touched her in ways that seemed dangerous at first, then became automatic and necessary. I lifted her shirt, heart thundering at the view, and stroked her and kissed the dark rings at each tip, took an entire breast into my mouth. She tugged her shirt off over her head, underarms white, vulnerable looking, and sloping to shoulder and breast in that smooth exciting connection that makes every part of a girl's body look delicious. I got some cat hair on my lips and had to stop and take it off. I asked Margie where she learned all the things she was doing.

She moved a hand to my shirt and dipped each button out of its slot, opened the shirt and pulled me against her. She whispered, "I read Mama's copy of *The Sensuous Woman*."

Completely lost now, I pressed my middle against hers, thrilled that she ground back against me, all the time running my hands over her soft rounded chest and the cotton panties at her hips where the dress had hiked. I shifted, ran my hand down the front of her miniskirt, Margie staring up at me like a victim, mouth wide, belly muscles jumping, and then, with my heart threatening to kill me, I placed my hand in the shockingly soft, hot, damp pout between her legs. She closed her eyes, reached down and squeezed me through two layers of cloth.

I smelled her beneath the perfume now, an odd familiar scent that reminded me of baby powder. She pulled away from a kiss to pick some cat fuzz from her mouth. I found the elastic of her panties and slid my hand under and down into the short coarser hair, the plump junction of thighs, belly, and ass, and my finger slipped across the hot slippery mouth, unbelievable to me in its hungry warmth, and then inside of her. Margie moaned and unsnapped my jeans, yanked the zipper and tugged my underwear down and wrapped her fingers around me, pumping. "Not quite so hard," I said, breathlessly, "and a little faster." With her other hand she guided the heel of my hand against her, above my plunging finger, and I understood to press small circles there.

"Easier," she whispered into my mouth. "Not so fast at first."

I was all heart and blood and motion. Our mouths sucked together, hands working each other's secret middles, making us breathe harder, sweating now, Margie exhaling little noises like a dove, me forgetting to be quiet as I felt the sweetness rising, her hand moving faster, and then I was dissolving from the center outward because of her, my body moving by itself, shuddering, as she pushed loose flesh up and down over my veiny stiffness, and I felt the trickle burning towards her fingers, and then I grasped her elbow to stop her because it was too much, almost hurting, and I suffered momentary shame, like wetting the bed, which passed when I saw how excited it made her.

For several sleepy, thirsty minutes, I continued to kiss her and stroke her with my finger, her cries shrinking higher, and then she thrashed and moaned loudly into my mouth and I felt my sliding finger gripped in slipperiness, and she shuddered and lay there panting, shivering.

The room seemed very warm. We kissed for a while, told each other I love you. The cat vibrated against my thigh.

An urgent bladder and sponge-dry mouth woke me in the night, and when I realized where I was, my stomach sparked and my eyes scraped open. Alert on the surface, I was slack at the core, as if some vital string had been cut, couldn't tighten. Margie breathed slowly beside me.

Something moved in the corner beside the bookcase. I raised only my head, jugulars pulsing, stomach muscles gathering with a twitch of the hernia, and watched a woman sneaking along the shadows flatten beside the closed door. With a drowsy anxiety, I supposed Margie's mother had come home, discovered us, and was trying to escape unnoticed. I lowered my head and pretended sleep, deciding to creep out at dawn so that this whole night would have the quality of a dream, something one could dismiss without too much worry. A guilty hangover was already parodying the evening's dizziness. I heard no movement. And then it occurred to me, a feeling like a scalpel inserted into my belly and dragged upwards, slitting me open, that this was the ghost.

I regulated my breathing, ignored my body, hid deep in my own mind. In imitating sleep I must've drifted back into it, because before long the earth rolled over and stuck a headache sun in my face and I remembered it all again, but the woman was gone and the door, in the blue prelight, was still latched. Maybe I hadn't been awake the first time. The things that live in your mind are as real as anything else.

I was in love with the girl beside me. I was in danger of being kicked out of school, planning crimes to prevent it. I tensed awake in the sharpening sunlight, so alive I could barely stand it.

I wanted to stay in Margie's room forever.

I wanted to get out of there as fast as I could, back to the safety of my friends.

Another Color

I leaned over to help Tim unfold one of the tents and my nausea slid, stomach to head, like poison in a test tube. I sat down fast, sweating, in the monkey-high grass of the Sullivans' backyard, my senses so wide open I smelled the staleness of my own sneakers.

Wade tugged nylon up into a sudden tent-shape, like opening a pop-up book, and said, "Margie wore him out. He can't even stand up." He giggled, voice higher than what he allowed for talking.

Joey O'Connor grinned bashfully, tossed another stake beside a corner of the tent, and Rusty set the stake in an eyelet and sank it with two hatchet blows, then shifted to the next one Joey had thrown. "They didn't do nothin but watch TV, so he claims."

"If you failed at sin," Tim said, "we still deserve to know specifics."

I moaned. The grass around me was bristling, and when I looked at the white clapboards of the garage, they bristled too. My hands tingled. It felt like punishment for last night.

Tim said, "Buddy, you ought to be eating grass like a dog. I puked earlier and I feel fine now."

I crawled to the bushes and pressed a finger to the root of my tongue, causing that throat-clutching convulsion that feels like the last horror before death. My body squeezed, overheated, and I urped fiery juices, felt better, got sick again like a spigot, hernia wrenching, and then spit strings for a while. The air seemed cooler then. I knee-walked into the bluish gloom of an almost finished tent, laid down, and then I heard myself snoring before I was quite asleep.

✝

When I came out of the tent, I drank lots of water from the hose.

We readied our bikes, oiling, tightening, pumping air. Wade tied his pack onto his handlebars, and Joey hung his on his sissy-bar. Tim unscrewed his blowgun into two pieces and taped them to the bike frame alongside his machete. Rusty had an English Racer (the rest of us drove Spiders), and he loaded his supplies into the totebags on each side of the rear fender.

We squatted into the old clubhouse to initiate Joey. Tim produced a picture of Saint Anthony, one of those wallet cards the school distributed on feast days. He persuaded Joey to poke his finger with a pin and scrawl his initials on the card with blood. Rusty read the ceremony out of a paperback book which purported to give the actual Mafia swearing-in formula. Tim held a lighter to the card as Joey parroted the oath, and our surrounding faces flickered green from the burning ink. Rusty pronounced him a member, and we all slapped Joey's back. He actually looked proud.

We wasted the rest of the afternoon playing Hide the Belt, which resulted in beatings as painful as the ones I got from Daddy, but somehow it seemed hilarious when done in the name of sport.

Around seven, Mr. Sullivan stoked the grill and left us to cook our own hot dogs. In the cooling dusk, surrounded by friends and meat smoke, crickets purring, birds roosting, my hangover passed completely away and left me happy. On the grill, my hot dog split with its own sizzling juices, and I speared it off and worked it into a toasted bun squiggled with red and yellow. We chewed like savages. The smoky meat tasted delicious.

Mr. Sullivan wandered out wearing shorts and a luau shirt stenciled with volcanoes and pineapples. He carried four beers and some cups over to the tray beside the grill, then popped the cans and poured about half of each into a cup. We looked at one another. Mr. Sullivan said, "We'll just pretend this is Europe." We thanked him desperately, as if we'd arrived from across a desert, then took small, responsible sips. Mr. Sullivan took a mustache-frosting chug from the can he'd reserved for himself and said, "I think I'll mosey on in and watch "All in the Family" with Linda. You all are welcome inside if you get tired of the wilderness."

"Thanks anyway," said Tim.

Mr. Sullivan walked up onto the porch and said, "Please don't pee in the vegetable garden, fellas. That's the cat's job." He wiped his feet and went inside.

"Wow," said Rusty. "Your dad's cool as hell."

"When we have company."

Tim convinced us to pour a mouthful of beer onto the ground as an offering to the gods, before we left for our mission.

I strapped my canvas bookbag on. We set out on our bikes, without hurry, gliding serpentine between the curbs. Passing a cluster of young women, Wade reared up his bike and rode half a block on the back tire. Rusty steered without hands. We felt dangerous and invulnerable, like a small army, like Hell's Angels.

We rode laughing into a usually idyllic neighborhood. But the elderly couples were not in their porch swings, and the younger ones weren't pushing their baby strollers or pulling Irish setters. We heard a nearby chanting, like a pep rally, and saw that a crowd was passing a few blocks ahead.

"What's that?" Joey asked, stopping and bracing out with one foot.

"The protest march," said Tim. "It was supposed to finish up at City Hall at eight."

"Spear-chunker parade," Rusty cracked.

Tim told him not to act retarded. "I don't want to cross through," he said. "It's like crossing a picket line, sort of."

"And I'm not in the mood to get beat up," I said.

"I don't think they'd harm us," Tim said. "But we'll just detour over a few blocks and avoid the whole thing."

Six blocks over we discovered a neighborhood of newly moved-in blacks and uneasy rednecks whose leases hadn't yet expired. A white woman stood on her porch shrieking at a black woman holding a baby across the street. Our gang clustered. A police car prowled past the end of the block, escorting the marchers. The city's population was fifty-fifty, black and white, and it looked like most of the black people were marching and most of the whites were locked up in their houses.

"We're gonna have to cross through them," Rusty said. "Might as well get it over with."

We coasted to the intersection and stopped. Rows of black people filed past, singing and shouting. Cars had stopped all along the intersecting streets. On the hood of a stranded Mustang, a thick-armed white boy sat drinking beer and glaring at the marchers. They were singing "We Shall Overcome" or chanting "No more lynching!" Some, though, were laughing and yelling, taunting the few white onlookers. Some of the male marchers were drinking from bagged cans or bottles. I heard the standard racial insults and the word "motherfucker" repeated.

A gangly black man leaned out of the crowd into my face, and I flinched back, and he said, "Give me five dollars, white boy!" I stared. I hadn't had five dollars at one time since my last birthday. He said it again and threw out his open hand. A tiny woman took hold of his shirt and pulled him along, singing. Rusty and Wade rode around the corner along the sidewalk to see how far the crowd extended. These looked mostly like stragglers and troublemakers. Maybe the serious people had gone home. I looked over at Tim. An older black kid with plaited hair had a grip on his handlebars and another was circling around behind the bike.

"Go on," Tim whined. "I already told you no."

"For real, brother," said the one behind him, and he sniffed like he had a cold. "Me and my partner need to rest our feet a minute. You my tight-man, ain't it?"

Tim said, "Let go, man. I'm not stupid enough to let you steal my bike and I've never done anything to deserve this shit."

The one in front stuck his chest out. "You think all a nigger can do is steal, is it?"

The rear one sniffed. "We done axed you nice, now, motherfucker. Hop off the motherfuckin bike or I'll help you off."

Tim's jaw was clenched and his eyes were glistening. I was boiling with outrage. Our teachers, my parents, and Tim had taught me to think of black people as disadvantaged by history. After a while you began to think of them as a martyred, saintly race, and this was easy enough to sustain because there were only a couple of dozen black kids at Blessed Heart, and only a few black guests at our parents' parties, and they were middle-class educated people with good intentions and a sense of themselves as ambassadors. But to believe that all black people were virtuous and fair seemed as ignorant to me as thinking they were all demons. Poor and desperate people are subject to all the ugliness that poverty bequeaths them. Plenty of blacks hated whites indiscriminately, and were violent, foulmouthed, and cruel. Color doesn't make people predictable. I was always sorry when I forgot that.

I saw no way out of our situation, which was complicated by feeling a complex and foolish sort of pity for these two boys. We could fight them, flee, or give them what they wanted, but whichever we did, they had already won. And any violence in this instance would likely be drastic. The boy behind Tim must've seen the fury and frustration in my face.

He sniffed. "What you got to say about it, pussy?"

Rusty and Wade straddled over on their bikes, and Rusty said, "What's the problem?" and left his mouth open like an animal.

They said there wasn't any problem, that Tim was lending them his bike. The one with the cold told Rusty to put his hands in his pockets. Rusty didn't do it, but because he wasn't yelling or calling them niggers I knew he was scared too.

Tim said, "What do you think it feels like to be surrounded by people of another color yelling names at you, trying to take your property and threatening to hurt you?"

The front one, with corn-row hair, said, "Seem to me like it's y'alls turn," and the one in back chuckled, leaned forward, and they slapped palms.

Tim said, "Shit, man, I've always been for civil rights. Ease up."

They both laughed at him, though it seemed forced, lots of exaggerated shrugging. Then the one with the sniffles said, "Where you was, Civil Rights, when they shot that young boy?" and the one in front said, "Right on, brother." I felt like everybody was attempting to speak in some mutual phony language.

Rusty said, "Don't talk to these fuckheads."

"Say what?" said the one in front.

Wade tightened all his muscles into scary knots and barked, "Fuck you!" and a white woman, marching past, held her fist up and shouted at us, "Racist pigs!"

I wished for the proverbial machine gun. I would've killed everybody around us, solved the whole goddamn problem. And then a girl walked by holding a framed picture of the Kennedys and Martin Luther King, and I had to remind myself for the thousandth time that everybody was a separate person.

I looked for Joey, didn't see him. At the next street over, a car was honking, creeping through the crowd. Marchers swarmed it. A man in cutoff slacks leaped onto the hood and started casually bouncing dents into the metal, the car bucking on its shocks. Another man dived onto the roof. There was a breaking of glass, a flash of light. The men jumped off the car and the crowd regrouped, a wedge of men tipping the car up onto two wheels.

The boy yanked up on Tim's handlebars, nearly jarring him off the bike, then did it again while he was off balance. Tim grabbed the boy's wrists. The other one sprang a headlock on me. Wade and Rusty dropped their bikes and came over and Wade got my attacker in a headlock too. My neck bones clicked.

A boy broke out of the crowd shouting, "Hey! Hey! What it is, brothers, what it is?" He pulled at the shoulder of the boy struggling with Tim. I was seeing this sideways through elbows. Wade backed off, the boy released my head.

The new arrival was Craig Dockery, our nemesis from Blessed Heart. We greeted him by name though, as if that made us acceptable to all blacks.

"Check it out," said the guy with plaited hair. "We was marching, right? And then he rides up screaming 'Kill niggers' and reachin for this knife." He pointed at Tim's untouched machete. We all shrieked, "Bullshit!"

Craig laughed and looked at us, then back at the other two. "For real? Naw, you jivin me, my man. Tiny Tim don't use that language. Now this one here might could've." He thrust his chin towards Rusty. "You get him pissed-off. They all right, man. They my school friends." Craig was talking street style, not the way he did at school. He held his hand out to me. His lip was still swollen from my fist, and my eye was still bruised from his. I

gave him a stiff, wary soul-shake—thumb around thumb, sliding into a finger clasp, fist tapping hand-backs, then release—
a ritual that always seemed too elaborate to be heartfelt. I can't
say I ever liked Craig, but at that moment, from a complex
emotional distance, I was so grateful I could've wept.

We heard a whomp! and saw that the upturned car was back
on all four wheels and scooting jerkily away, the crowd laughing.

"Man, you actin the Tom," said the sniffler.

"Everybody got to live together," said Craig. "One night y'all
might be in *their* neighborhood."

The boys sucked their teeth and sulked off, muttering about
motherfuckers. We collected onto our bikes. Tim thanked Craig,
and Rusty managed a grudging "Preciate it."

"Some of these street niggers ain't used to white folks," Craig
said. "Y'all mind yourselves. I want you healthy for Monday
when I whip your ass." He rejoined the crowd, showed us a
carnivorous smile, sauntered away.

Joey crept out from the lee of a parked van, and we were
too upset to berate him. We excused ourselves humbly through
the marchers, walking our bikes. Some people scowled like they
wished us dead, others smiled and wished us "Good evening."

When we got across, we pedaled full-speed until Joey's lungs
stopped working, then swerved into a neighborhood park and
skidded up around a bench. Tim dug the bottle of sacramental
wine from his pack and unscrewed it, poked it into his mouth,
and threw his head back like a starved infant. Joey collapsed
across the seat of the bench, sucking air, belly heaving. We had
to pry the bottle away from Tim, less than half left to share
between the rest of us.

Bwana Tim

We rode past the Highway 80 Drive-In. Its glowing marquee announced *Pat Garrett and Billy the Kid* and *Super Fly T.N.T.,* but several of the letters had been subtracted and rearranged below to spell TITTY. The drive-in was so decadent that it allowed this to stand, lit up like Christmas, on its busiest night.

Rolling on through Thunderbolt, a subdivision on the Worthington River, we kept our conversation equal to the dark and quiet, but dogs began a barking relay, and in many houses a curtain swept back to reveal a concerned resident framed in light. A police car was approaching from down the road, moving slower than we were. We turned into one of the marinas, watched some swaying fishermen hang a barracuda on the scales at the dock, then slipped out the other gate, behind the cruiser now.

Most of the driveways we passed contained trailered boats, usually beside a Mercedes or Cadillac. "Try and look rich," Rusty advised.

We pedaled up two bridges and coasted down them, then swung onto the small road to Marshland Island and followed Tim into the trees.

We traded snacks and ate them, more for ceremony than

from hunger. All spicy, the mixture grumbled in your belly. We watched by flashlight as Joey nibbled the meat off a pig's foot. It had intact toenails. I wasn't tempted to sample it.

Still munching, we opened the shoe polish applicators and painted one another's faces, daubing leafy smudges with the wet foam tips, exchanging earth colors. The smell made me dizzy, watery-eyed, like breathing gasoline fumes. Rusty held a flashlight on us, watching.

Tim said, "Shew!" and shined his light in each of our faces. "We look pretty good. But you guys stand out because of your arms and necks."

"I don't want this stuff on my arms," Wade moaned. "It stinks."

"I volunteer," I said, feeling so soiled already I figured it might as well be complete.

After painting our arms we went all the way and ruined our T-shirts too, except for Wade, who was wearing a camouflage tank top, and Tim, who had borrowed his dad's fatigue shirt. It hung on him like a smock. His long blond hair was a giveaway, but I didn't mention it.

"All right," Rusty said finally, as if we'd worn him down with pestering. "I guess you better camouflage me too."

I marked him up like foliage, one color at a time, quick and spotty.

"This is our last night of gangsterism," said Tim, digging into his pack. "Now is a good time to eat those Eucharists."

He divided them up and we ate them, crisp first, then mushy, bland but magical. I'd never had more than four in a week.

Then crackling gravel and the whir of an engine stopped us. We killed our lights, swallowed our mouthfuls, touched one another in the dark. Headlights burned past, white beams containing insects and engine smoke, leading the silhouette of a truck. Music thumped and sloshed from its open windows.

Out of sight, the truck paused at the entrance to the compound, music slightly louder as a door clunked open. Chains

165

tinkled, hinges shrieked. We guessed the gate was being opened. The truck revved, stopped again, and after more sounds of metal on metal, zoomed out of earshot. We stayed quiet for a minute. Small wild animals began to stir in the undergrowth around us. Claws scritched on pine bark. A hand clamped my elbow, activating the funny bone, and Joey said, "What the hell was that?" Everyone shushed him.

Tim whispered, "It's just a raccoon or a possum or something."

"What are we going to do?" I asked. "That truck's inside now."

"Doesn't make a shitlick of difference," Rusty said aloud. "They ain't gonna be near the animals this time of night."

"That's true," Tim said, flipping his flashlight on and scanning the area. "Okay, let's finish getting ready. We'll leave the bikes here."

I held a light on Tim while he assembled his blowgun and hung it by its strap across his back. We threaded the machete scabbards onto our belts. I felt altogether safe and powerful, because of our collective cunning, strength, and weaponry. From the chattering, laughing, and cursing of the others, I knew they felt it too.

"We're ready," Tim said. "Anybody want to say anything?"

"Yeah," said Rusty. "This wasn't my idea." He laughed.

"Hold on a second," Joey said. "I need to use the bathroom. Did anybody bring toilet paper?"

"Tim's usually got a pocketful of snot rags," Rusty said.

"I need them for my allergies," said Tim. "You ought to plan ahead, Joey. Here." He unfurled a wadded banner of tissue from his pocket and tore some off for Joey.

Wade said, "I need to take a leak."

We all turned around and took a few steps and began to empty ourselves.

"Hey," said Tim over a pattering palmetto, "does anybody else's urine come out in two separate streams when you first start, then join together?"

166

"Nuh," said Rusty. "You got a disease."

I said mine did occasionally. We made zipping noises, and Rusty called, "You about finished, Joey?"

From behind an oak, Joey snapped, "Don't rush me! I feel bad!" followed by a vile noise that you felt awful laughing at, but couldn't help.

We skirted the fence through the woods around to where the marsh began. There was a half-circle inlet on our right that ended in a wooden footbridge joining the woods trail to a loop of trail through the marsh. Across the river a few yellow porch lights shone. Our camouflage worked surprisingly well in the gloom. I could barely make out my friends' shapes against the trees, except for Tim's albino hair.

Rusty turned his flashlight on the marsh. "Now, we can slop through the marsh all the way around this little bay, or we can wade right across to that footbridge. That'll save time and mess."

Joey said, "Let's go back to the road and climb the fence."

"Sure," Tim said. "Joey, I'd pay money to see you clamber over that barbed wire." He pulled a trail map out and directed a circle of light over our route. "This dock-bridge leads right onto a trail."

"This water isn't going to hurt us any more than that damn shoe polish did," said Wade. "What's the big deal?"

"Yeah, you go first," said Tim.

The intervening marsh grass crackled like a roll of caps afire, so we went slowly to lessen the noise. River mud slurped at our shoes, the sound of flushed toilets. A pattering like rain beside us prompted my flashlight on, revealing a side-stepping square yard of fiddler crabs ticking towards their muddy holes. A few of the big ones challenged us, raising their single oversized claws.

We slogged to the end of the reeds, the mud deepening, getting slicker. Water ran into our shoes, provoked cursing. Joey fell and sank backward in a bed of muck. He turned over, trying to get up, smearing his belly with mud too. We had to help him. Tim took the lead into the water, lighting the way.

We waded towards the bridge. I took off my backpack, in case the water got too deep, so it wouldn't get wet.

"This water's cold," Tim said. "It hurts."

"It ain't that bad," said Rusty.

"You're taller. All of you. The water's right on a level with my privates. They're all drawn up from the coldness."

"I could carry you piggyback," Wade volunteered.

"No, I can handle it. I just want you all to know I'm suffering more than anyone else here."

A few steps from the footbridge, something smashed the water like a tossed log. We squealed curses, Tim screaming, "Don't move! Don't move!" and we froze there and Joey halted across from us where he was trying to scramble up into the marsh. I smelled boy-sweat, shoe polish, river mud.

"What is it?" we said.

"Shh."

I remembered my machete, got it into my hand. Tim heard my blade sliding out of canvas and unsheathed his too. Rusty and Wade produced knives. Joey climbed another grass-crackling step onto land. Tim's flashlight ignited a pair of eyes floating on the water just ahead of him. His light began to jiggle.

"Oh . . . my God!" He sounded like someone was pounding his back. "It's a . . . huge . . . alligator."

"You sure?" asked Rusty quietly.

The gator's mouth opened, top jaw breaking water with a hiss like a flattening tire, the pale pink mouth wide, dripping water from ripsaw teeth. Joey groaned from the sidelines. Rusty wheezed. Wade, retreating, bumped into me. The mouth closed gradually, eyes vigilant, the same style of movement as a snake.

Tim, in a pained insect voice, said, "Take out your flashlights, slowly, and shine them right in his eyes . . . hurry, Jesus Christ."

Wade, Rusty, and I turned our beams on and the gator sank to eyeballs and nostrils again. Then, from the bank beside us, Joey's tardy light illuminated us all for the reptile to see.

"Turn it off, Joey!" I whispered. "You're too far!" My knees were thudding each other underwater.

Tim passed his flashlight to Rusty, the beam still aimed at the eyes, and Rusty took it alongside his own light. Tim eased the blowgun from his shoulder and held it towards the gator, machete poised in the other hand.

"I'm going to try to . . . nudge him away," Tim quavered. "If he comes at me—" he released a tortured breath, "—you all please . . . don't let him kill me."

He lowered the tip of the blowgun towards the gator's submerged shoulder. Wade pressed back against me. The camouflaged tube entered the water. A membrane slid over the gator-eyes. Tim thrust the blowgun.

The creek exploded. The great armored tail raised a geyser. Tim slashed, screaming, and we clustered, shouted, floundered towards the bridge. Wade's flashlight plunked, lit the grayish murk, winked out. I flung a water-heavy leg onto the bridge and pulled myself up, saw Tim struggling to climb with his blowgun and machete in hand, and I dragged him up too, at great cost to my hernia. Wade thumped down beside us. Rusty hurried over from the near bank where he'd fled, shoes packed in five pounds each of mud. Blundering towards us through the grass like a wounded hippo, Joey gasped, "Where is it? Where'd it go?"

A panther's roar rumbled from across the island. I felt besieged by man-eating animals, a pioneer in the Georgia jungles.

"Oh my God," Tim groaned, lying on his back. He repeated this over and over. Nobody was hurt.

169

✝

We convalesced on the footbridge for ten minutes, rising from the waist in giddy terror at every natural sound.

"Well," Rusty said, "we ain't coming out the way we came in, that's for damn sure."

"He was more scared of us than we were of him," Tim said.

"Then he's probably dead of a heart attack," Joey sneered.

I studied the heavens. The deeper I looked, the more stars revealed themselves, until the sky seemed composed of a grayish wash of smaller and smaller lights. A shooting star sparkled across the sky and everybody's finger went up at once.

Then I said, "Do y'all reckon that gator escaped from its pen, or was it wild?"

"Wild," Tim said. "But I wouldn't feel any safer in the water with a tame one. Man-oh-man!"

"You can easily hold their mouths shut," said Wade. "They bite down with hundreds of pounds of pressure, but they've only got about five pounds worth of opening pressure."

"Well why didn't you subdue him then?" Rusty said. From his tone, I knew he had his skeptical eyebrows raised.

"I didn't think of it at the time," said Wade. "I saw a guy do it at an alligator farm in Florida, though."

"I can't take all this in one night," Joey said. "How about if I stay here on the bridge and keep a lookout for trouble."

Tim said, "Joey, I want you to act like a tough guy, now. Just think, the next time some kid calls you a fatass you can remember that you confronted an eight-foot-long alligator in its element. That'll give you the courage to smear him."

Rusty insisted the gator was no more than five feet long. "Maybe less. Everything looks big to you because you're so small," he said.

"Listen, I've gotten straight A's in Math for eight years and I say it was eight feet long. Can you prove it wasn't?"

"I'm too tired to go on," Joey whined. Secretly, I empathized. I felt slightly homesick and miserable myself. I missed my bed, but saying it would only make it worse. I didn't dare think of Margie.

Tim said, "Everybody who thinks we should throw Joey to the river creatures, say 'Aye.'"

It was unanimous. But we agreed to spare him if he stopped complaining.

Banshee in the Woods

What's that?" I said, stopping on the trail. I heard a sort of magnified heartbeat through the trees.

"Calypso music," Joey said. "Reggae. I think it's coming from that same truck we saw earlier."

"We'd better investigate," said Tim.

We crept along the trail. When the woods began to thin out, we pocketed our flashlights and relied on the moon. We stopped at the trees' end, trail's exit.

The truck was parked at the edge of a field, near the pens for the farm animals and a barn. Out in the center of the field two figures sat in the grass while an oceanic rhythm and mumbly lyrics burbled from the truck. Smoke twisted in the moonlight above their heads, and a red dot floated between them, glowed, floated, then flared, lighting a bearded face and the long hair, shoulder, and bare back of a woman.

"They're butt naked!" Tim said. "I think they are."

"Smells like they're smokin dope," said Rusty.

I said, "It's that guy Paul who showed us around the island."

We moved closer, quailing at every snapped twig or crunched leaf, though surely the music overpowered our noise. A few feet from the truck, which screened us from the field, Tim dug a flat metal box from his pack. He pressed a button and it snapped open into a pair of field glasses. He put them to his eyes and his mouth dropped open.

"She's sexy as hell," he whispered. "Who wants to rent my opera glasses? Fifty cents per minute."

Rusty and Wade both snatched at the glasses. Rusty got them, looked, and said, "God almighty." They took turns, exclaiming mildly. Wade, grinning, passed me the glasses. Mostly, they magnified the grainy haze and shadows, but whenever the nudists inhaled on the joint, I saw reddish details. Paul was muscled like a comic-book hero, his penis alert out of the lotus position. The woman was younger and had hair down to her waist, and she was rocking in time to the music. Her breasts weren't much larger than Paul's, but even in this gloom I saw that her nipples did a spectacular job of compensation. She was not entirely naked— she still wore panties. I shouldn't be here, I thought. I should be with Margie again.

And though I had lately smoked marijuana and spent the night with a girl, I was somehow disappointed to see Paul behaving the same way. I'd admired him, a big impressive man and champion of wilderness. I preferred my heroes to be nobler than me. Sexuality still worried me as much as it made me excited. I have never stopped being shocked that respectable people with jobs and families would peel their clothes off and indulge in the mutual friction which in public would get them arrested. I handed the binoculars to Joey.

As Joey watched in close-up, the couple finished smoking and leaned into a long writhing kiss, her hair swinging forward, his hands rising to her breasts, and then her head dipped down into his lap and began to rise and fall. He leaned over her and began rubbing her ass.

"Jesus, Mary, and Joseph," Rusty said and took the glasses from Joey.

We stared for a minute in fascinated agony, ashamed to look at one another. I felt I had a tennis ball jammed in my pants.

"Let's go," Tim said. "I'm sick of watching other guys have what I want."

"Hold it a second," said Rusty. "This ain't somethin you can see just anytime."

"Give me my field glasses, damn it. Let's go let that cat out while these two are occupied."

We walked stiffly around the field's perimeter, blending against the trees, and found the continuation of the trail. In two minutes we were up on the viewing platform over the bobcat pen. It seemed we'd gotten there too quickly. I didn't feel ready.

"We'll never feel ready," Tim said. "We just have to do it any-way. Now, find me a wildcat." He put the field glasses to his face.

We turned on our lights (except Wade, who'd drowned his) and swept their beams through the enclosed woods. I was tense and had to make myself stop clenching my teeth too hard. I lifted my beam up into the large oak tree, to the claw-scoured limb where we'd seen a bobcat on the field trip. I traced the limb back and forth with light and was about to look elsewhere when I imagined that a bulge on the limb was a cat, decided it wasn't, then saw it raise its head. "Found one," I whispered, holding him in the light. He blinked.

"I see it!" Joey said.

"Joey sees it," Wade mocked, but he was grinning up at it too.

Tim loaded a dart into the mouthpiece. He inhaled, put his lips to it, then pulled away. "Wait! wait, damn. I almost ruined everything. If I dart that bobcat in the tree, he'll either fall and break his neck or else he'll go to sleep up there and we'll have hell getting him down."

Rusty turned his flashlight onto a bush to the left of us and squinted. "I thought I saw one in here a minute ago." Rusty waved the light a little. "See? Ain't that a pair of cat eyes?"

Two glints floated in the leaves, caught light like marbles.

"Yeah," said Wade. "It just moved."

"Eureka," said Tim. "I'll simply estimate where the rump is and put him under."

We lined up along the railing above the fence. Rusty, Joey, Wade, and I jacklighted the hidden bobcat. Tim took a breath and aimed, then jerked back like it had stung him.

"Wait a second," he said, frowning. He spit, rubbed his eyes, and shook out each hand, shifting the weapon. He sighed, then lifted the blowgun and readied himself again. He filled his cheeks. He stared at the bush, not breathing.

Tim's cheeks hollowed with a hiss. The bush shook violently and a cat sprang from each side of it, one slipping straight into an adjacent bush, the other pouncing and snarling up along the chicken-wire fence, a yellow dart-cone stuck to its haunch.

The cat leapt into the hollowed-out front of a stump. Tim lowered the blowgun and leaned limply against the railing. "Perfect shot," he said. "I can't begin to tell you how hard that was on me."

"Now what?" Joey asked.

"We get things ready while we wait for the drug to take hold. Wade, let's hang that rope, man."

After several tosses Wade got the rope over the nearest limb of the oak tree, but we couldn't retrieve the dangling end, even using the blowgun to hook it, in order to fasten it. The bobcat in the tree paced and growled. Finally we pulled the rope back and tied it to the railing so that it hung down inside the fence.

"Nothing ever works out as spectacular as you want it," Tim said, yanking to test the knot. "It's not Robin Hood, but I guess it'll work. We'll leave the rope here to convince them we really did it."

"What about fingerprints?" Joey asked.

"I don't think they can take fingerprints off this rope. I wore gloves when I made the notes."

"Anyhow," Rusty said, "our fingerprints ain't on file."

"But if they suspected us," I said, "then they might take our fingerprints."

"So what?" Rusty said. "This ain't mass murder. It's about the same as stealin the mascot from the enemy football team."

Tim said, "We'll shift that critter to the outside, go deliver the notes, and bust a window, then get drunk and watch the sun come up in my backyard."

Tim, wearing leather work gloves, stapled a note to the railing, a patchwork of letters and words sliced out of newspapers. He put one foot over the rail and rested it on the top of the fence, gripped the rope, paused, and stepped back onto the deck. "Wade, since you're biggest, you go on down first. I want to see what those other cats do. Take my machete." He unsheathed it and gave it to Wade. "I'll keep you covered with the blowgun."

Wade hopped over and slid down the rope. He stood and turned in a circle and looked up at us, white eyes in a leafy face, and shrugged.

Tim laid down the blowgun. "Now for the easy part," he said, and slipped down the rope and landed in a crouch, swashbuckler style. He threw his hands onto his hips and looked around, tried to spit but only produced the noise. His dad's fatigue shirt hung on him like a cape, and his hair waved around the shadowy pen like a flag of surrender. "You all keep your lights trained on those other cats until we're out of here. Rusty, we'll hand him up to you."

I lit the treed bobcat pacing angrily on his limb. He slowed, tail switching. Joey, unable to discover the third cat, played his light around the habitat like a prison guard spotlighting from a tower.

Tim handed his flashlight to Wade and crept towards the hollow stump. He squatted in front of it, and for a moment the night was so quiet I heard his knees click. Wade stood alongside, shining the light for him, machete raised.

A growl upset the silence, and I said, "Watch it!" and Tim fell back, looking everywhere, and Wade raised the machete higher.

176

"It was only my stomach!" Joey said defensively. "It was my stomach growling."

"Sorry," I said, and giggled nervously.

Tim stood before the stump again and said over his shoulder, "Rusty, that five bucks you owe me. If I get killed, give it to Francis so he can take Margie to the movies."

"If the cat kills you," Rusty said, "I'll use that five bucks to get him stuffed and put in the trophy case at school."

Tim chuckled, then lifted his foot and eased the toe into the hole of the stump. He nudged. Then he squatted again and put both hands inside. I was wincing, teeth gritted with anxiety. Then Tim stood and turned, a sagging bobcat in his arms, its tongue out.

We said, "All right!" and "Son of a bitch!" and laughed, finally surprised that the Wildcat Caper had succeeded. I believed then that we were capable of anything.

Tim plucked the dart from the cat's hide and its tongue slid up into the mouth and it swallowed.

Rusty said, "He's alive all right."

"Wade," Tim said, "take this dart and wipe the prints off of it, then lay it down where they'll be sure to find it. Also, see if you can locate some bobcat droppings and stick them in the baggie."

Wade stuck the machete in the ground and wiped the dart on his shirt.

Tim looked at the cat in his arms and held it up at me. "Did he who made the lamb make thee?" He grinned.

"William Blake," I said.

Tim looked at the cat's underside. "Hey, this is a female."

I glanced up at the oak limb where I'd been holding the light, but the bobcat had disappeared. I lit the other limbs, suspicious bulges, clusters of leaves. I heard an exhalation below.

Tim's painted face was turned up at me, mouth stretched, forehead squeezed, and his hands were up behind his neck. The limp bobcat lay in the grass. Tim's knee buckled and he half turned. The other bobcat was on his shoulders, jaw clamped at

177

the base of his skull. I threw light on him. Wade looked over from the far side of the pen. I shouted as loud as I could and felt my hernia tearing open, and from the top of the oak tree a huge white heron rose and flapped slowly into the darkness.

Rusty leapt into the pen, hitting the ground hard. I threw myself onto the rope and slid down it, my insides tearing more with the effort and bulging into my pants, and I fell to the ground and kneeled up and screamed at the cat as it jerked Tim's neck and Rusty and Wade kicked at it.

The cat pounced away. Wade pulled the machete out of the ground. We watched, in the trembling pool of Joey's flashlight, as Tim's eyes shifted panicky from Rusty to Wade to me, then lost focus and drifted. I found I was holding my hand against the pain in my groin and praying for Tim not to die. We stayed there confused.

"Bring him up!" Joey shouted. "Get out of there!"

We looked around for the cats. There was electricity around my heart, but I was hurt too bad to escape quickly.

Rusty said, "Wade! Get up there and I'll hand him up to you. Joey, shit, I guess you better go get that guy and tell him what happened." He spun his light around the enclosure.

"What if they're still screwing?" Joey said, and turned and ran into the woods where the trail was.

"We're in big trouble," Rusty said. "Help me get him up."

"I can't," I gasped, and even the effort of speaking stabbed at my groin. "My hernia's busted wide open."

Rusty slung Tim over his shoulder and passed him up to Wade. Then they did the same to me. I felt terribly weak and was glad to surrender myself to stronger people.

I sat on the deck with my knees pulled up tight against me, beside Tim. I prayed helplessly. I counted six little punctures on the back of his neck. There was some blood, but I'd seen him lose much more than that in fights and still be able to laugh at it. I stared down at the planking between my shoes. I didn't look at

Tim after that. Rusty tore the note off of the railing and stuffed it in his pocket.

I heard an eerie voice in my head, like the voice of my adult self in years to come, scolding me: Now you've done it, boy. Now you've really done it.

Paul Steatham crashed out of the woods with a lantern flashlight and thundered up onto the platform, squeezed Tim's throat, and said, "The ambulance is coming." Then Joey appeared with the girl. She said she'd opened the gate. She stood behind Paul, wearing a tie-dyed shirt now, hugging herself as if it was cold. Every few seconds someone coughed or sighed or called on God.

Paul said, "Let's carry him to the building to save time." He took Tim under the arms and lifted, and Rusty took his legs, and Wade supported him in the middle, and they carried him down the trail. I hobbled and gasped behind them.

"Are you hurt too?" the girl asked.

I said I was, a little. She held onto me, trying to help. It made it more awkward, but I was glad to have a woman's arms around me. We heard the siren of an ambulance wailing onto the island like a banshee in the dark.

The ambulance left as the girl and I came out of the woods and the police cars were pulling in. The gang was sitting on the porch of the building, between the giant white columns. Mr. Doolan, the policeman from our neighborhood, got out of one of the cars. Two other cops headed down the trail with Paul, carrying long flashlights. I watched all this from inside a thick, quiet

179

bubble. I was calm and shaking. Mr. Doolan came over, but he didn't recognize us with our faces painted. Rusty identified us.

Paul took us into the building to call our parents. I was hunched over and every step felt like a kick in the groin. Mr. Doolan saw and then helped me out to his patrol car and got in. He held the microphone to his mouth and told the dispatcher he was taking me to the emergency room. Suddenly I was afraid that this was the car I'd tossed the douche into a few days ago, and I regretted every wrong thing I'd ever done.

"Everything's gonna be okay, Francis," said Mr. Doolan. He shoved the car in gear and we heard popping noises from the woods, and my soul sank deeper into its terrible self. He turned on the siren and screamed towards the hospital at such speed that I was able to get scared again.

Underground

The hospital was near our neighborhood. Attendants were waiting at the curb with a wheeled stretcher, and my parents materialized as I was lying down. "We're here," Mama said, and followed beside us as I was rolled through the sliding glass doors. They behaved as if they'd done something wrong and needed me to forgive them.

In a curtained-off area in a white room, a black man wearing glasses helped me strip and wriggle into a gown. He tried to converse with me about baseball while he soaped me and shaved off my pubic hair. I looked down once and saw a bulge on the right side of my groin the size of an egg. Then the man put a tube inside me and filled me with liquid and slid a bedpan under me to take it back. A nurse entered and gave me a shot in the thigh that hurt beyond what I thought I could stand. She told me not to tense the muscle, to relax.

Men pushed me into a room lit brightly in the center, and placed me under the light, shining with steel, surrounded by darkness. I was cold. I kept my eyes closed. A nurse brought hot towels and spread them over me, and when they cooled she brought more. People gathered around me, and a man all in cloth except for eyeglasses and rubber gloves slipped a mask over my nose and mouth and I breathed a sweet, heavy gas. He told me to count backwards from ten, and I began to say the muffled numbers. Someone worked a needle with plastic wings into a vein on the back of my hand, taped it there, connected to a tube running up into a bag of clear liquid, hung from a metal gallows. I couldn't breathe. I felt sick, and I was going to tell them to take the mask away, and then everything grew numb and quiet except for a thudding inside my head.

Someone far away and invisible said, "It's all over, Francis. You're fixed and sewn up and ready to heal."

Later I heard women talking. I felt injured and nauseated and was moaning softly every few seconds. Someone laid a damp, cool cloth on my forehead. I was too sick to open my eyes and afraid to throw up because even the tiniest movement was like a knife plunging into me. I understood that the women talking, more quietly now, were nurses.

"D.O.A.?"

"Mm hmm. Had been, a while."

"It's awful to say," one whispered, "but it's probably for the best, with his spinal cord the way it was."

One walked over and pressed my wrist for several seconds. Something plastic was around my wrist, loose. She said, "You want some chipped ice to chew on, honey? It'll make you feel better. We can't give you anything else for pain yet."

All I could manage was a moan.

She placed something beside my head. "I'll leave this basin here in case you want to get sick." She walked away and sat down on a creaky metallic chair.

For a long while I stayed helpless in a delirium of nausea and pain, but I heard everything they said.

"You should've seen the flirt-face she gave Billy when he picked me up after the eleven-to-seven."

"She is a pure b-i-t-c-h."

My stomach pushed up into my throat and I grabbed for the basin and retched into it, turning painfully, the tube pulling at my hand. I gagged more, then swallowed a vile sourness. The nurse emptied the basin and gave me chipped ice in a washcloth. I sucked at it feebly, like an animal.

For days after the accident I felt sleepy and stupid and like I was wrapped all over in warm blankets. I hardly remember anything about the funeral. I had to wear my school uniform because I didn't have a suit, and I walked bent over where my flesh was tightened with prickly thread and stiff, iodine-stained bandages. The chapel was almost full with people I knew, and I tried to cry but I couldn't. I accidentally caught a glimpse of Tim's profile in the coffin, which was somehow confusing, because I had this notion that he was in the back somewhere, slouched against a wall and rolling his eyes like the patron saint of boredom. I'm sorry I saw him that last time, because I carried it with me for years—hair trimmed, not pale enough—like a touched-up souvenir photo.

On the way to the cemetery our Volkswagen stalled at a stoplight and Charles Sapp's daddy had to push us with his Impala.

We stood under a canopy held up with poles and when I sat down in the metal chair one leg sank into the ground so that I was tilted. The casket was lowered into the dirt on nylon straps between brass poles. I remembered that Tim had said if everybody that ever lived was buried, there wouldn't be room left on the earth for the living. When they began to shovel the mound onto him, I started to panic. What if he was in a coma and wasn't really dead, what if he woke up and found himself packed into solid darkness with only a few horrible hours of air left? I had to tell someone! They had to pull him back up and check, wait a few days. And then I remembered about embalming. That's when Tim really died for me.

An aunt of Tim's was there, a woman he'd once told me hated his guts, and she cried so hard that Tim's parents had to support her all the way down the hill into the black limousine.

I followed my parents slowly to the car, and my father was unlocking it when I noticed a pretty blonde girl in the distance, saw that she was looking at me, and then knew that it was Margie Flynn. She said something to her mother. My parents ducked into the smell of overheated plastic, and Margie ran towards me holding the hem of her white dress against her legs. I hadn't seen her since before. She was beautiful.

Margie hugged me and drew back and said, "Oh! Did I hurt you? I forgot." She looked at me and hugged me again, carefully, nice smelling and soft, the only pleasant thing I'd been conscious of for days. She said, "Call me whenever you feel like it," and, so my parents wouldn't hear, she moved her lips without sound, saying I love you.

She walked away then, turning back twice to wave. I could see her when I got home if I wanted. I realized that, and realized I wasn't dead. Tim was behind us, underground. I'd had it wrong for days. I got into the car and cried like I was having a seizure.

For a long time everyone was very, very nice to me.

Not Approved by the Comics Code Authority

The adventure actually had the effect we'd intended, though Tim's death crushed any possibility of satisfaction. We did not return to school after the accident, Kavanagh never again mentioned our comic-book obscenity, and Blessed Heart graduated us, though I didn't attend the ceremony. Our gang became legendary. The local TV stations sent crews to Marshland Island and interviewed Paul Steatham. There were wobbly close-ups of a stain on the wood of the observation platform, supposedly from Tim, and ominous shots of the empty bobcat pen. The cats had all been destroyed by the police. A group of citizens got very angry about that, and I agreed with them. It was our fault, not the bobcats'.

I spent so much lonely time in my room that summer that I became very good at drawing. That and Margie Flynn sustained me through the miseries of high school, after most of my friends had moved away. A couple of years ago I stopped in Tennessee to visit Rusty Scalisi, who was working for his father, running a contracting company. We got very drunk at a hamburger bar, and I suggested that if Tim was alive he'd either be some kind of folk-hero artist or a radical crusader. Rusty said, "He wouldn't be alive now, even if he hadn't gotten killed when he did. People like that die young. They have an influence on other people that lasts, but they don't." I was inspired by that observation to create a comic-book story about Tim.

Margie and I lasted through most of high school. Until I was seventeen, she was the only girl I had ever kissed, and I began to feel cheated a little, and suggested we date other people for a while. Most other girls were uninteresting after Margie, and I was thinking finally of asking her to marry me. But during our separation, which had sent her into a depression I still feel guilty about, she started dating a variety of men and didn't want to stop. When I suggested an engagement, she was going out simultaneously with a married forty-year-old bank manager and a baseball player who hit her when he was drunk. It became difficult even to stay friends. When we went off to different colleges, I heard she had gotten involved with an older girl, and I was so stunned by this at the time that I lost touch with her. By the time I'd gotten over it, there didn't seem to be any reason to get in contact with her. She's one of my biggest regrets. I'm still in love with her memory.

After art school I created an underground comic book called *The Dangerous Lives of Altar Boys,* about a group of teenage anarchists who battle hypocrisy, injustice, and eternal bullshit. Their leader is a long-haired skeleton with a halo, a boy who died and rose from the dead to remake the world the way he thought it should be. I got a lot of letters, unusual for an underground magazine. Most of them were from adults, and most of them were very encouraging. A few were shocked by the rough language and outrageous ideas and the drugs. I threw those away.

Last time I attended a comic-book convention in Atlanta, a man from DC Comics in New York came to my booth and asked me if I'd be interested in mass marketing *Altar Boys* now that the Comics Code Authority was dead and they could do whatever they wanted. I'm going up to sign a contract next month. I want people to see and hear the things I can see and hear. And I want them to remember how it was when they were children. I don't want them to grow up entirely.

Every adult is the creation of a child. My own signature, that identifying scrawl required by parcel postmen and valued by a handful of comic-book fans, that signature was devised by a thirteen-year-old boy who thought I'd want to seem important one day. I am stuck with it. My life is the result of that boy's dreams and limitations, and of the company that boy kept a long time ago, back when things could still happen for the first time.